THE CRADLE BREAKER

CONVENIENT WOMEN COLLECTION BOOK ONE

DELPHINE WOODS

PEPPER POT PUBLISHING

Created with Vellum

INSPIRED BY

Rock-a-bye baby,
on the treetops,
When the wind blows,
the cradle will rock,
When the bough breaks,
the cradle will fall,
And down will come baby,
cradle and all.

PART I

BONNIE

CHAPTER 1

August 1865

My mother named me Bonnie, for I was born on a Sunday. She told me this often when I was sulking, my lower lip jutting out. She would say, *I called you Bonnie, and I expect to see you act like it.* And then her hand, which always seemed so soft and weak in her husband's hands, would hit me, and it would be as hard as wood.

When I was little, I would cry after she'd hit me. But when I realised all I needed to do to make her happy – and so make myself happy – was smile, I smiled all the time. *Bonnie and blithe, good and gay.* I thought of that little rhyme as others thought of their bibles; I lived by it. I had a fixation for a few years, and I would ask anyone I met on which day they had been born, and I would decide if I liked them or not depending on their answer. Not many of them knew, of course, and so, after a little while of speaking with them, I would guess which day it had been.

I guessed when I saw her standing outside the house, the sea breeze catching at the loose hair which had escaped her bonnet, that Luella had been born on a Monday. Of course, I did not know her as Luella then. I was dusting in the drawing room, picking up all the stupid little knick-knacks, polishing them off, wiping away the tell-tale grey ring on the windowsill on which they sat, when I happened to straighten my back. I felt a sharp stab of pain after bending for so long and let my eyes rest on the view outside.

She gave me a bit of a fright standing on the edge of the green all in white, her skirts thin and cage-less and billowing in the wind. She looked how I imagined a ghost would look, how the novelists write them. But as she stared at me, I could see the prettiness of her: the blush on the pale of her cheeks, the structure of her bones underneath her flesh, the plump youthfulness of her skin. If I tell you to think of a pretty English girl, you will think of Luella. Monday, fair of face.

She watched me. The sun was high above her, and her white dress dazzled me. I had to blink and wipe the wetness from my eyes, and when I squinted down at her again, she was still staring at me, her face in the shade of her bonnet. She was gloveless, and her fists were clenched tight.

Behind her, women in twos walked on the green with prams or little short-nosed dogs on leads. Some of them noticed the strange girl, dressed so differently from themselves, but most of them did not glance in her direction. Behind them, Stowmouth's wattle-and-daub buildings shone, and its church spire rose into the blue sky like an arrow.

It felt like minutes had passed as we watched each other; in truth, now I think, it must only have been seconds. There was a noise somewhere below in the house – Cook, probably, chopping some dead animal's head off its body – and the sudden sound startled us both; she must have heard it through the opened windows. She dropped her gaze and looked to the floor, and the rim of her old-fashioned bonnet hid her face from me. Without looking at me again, she turned and strode away. She walked straight across the green and almost collided with a perambulator; the woman stopped short and said something, but I could only see the tight working of the woman's lips rather than hear the words. Luella did not falter. She continued to march until she reached Stowmouth's main streets where she vanished amidst the houses and shops.

I tried to dismiss the thought of her. I continued to dust as a bead of sweat dripped off the tip of my nose and splattered on a side table. I damned the heat, but it was not just the summer sunshine which had made me perspire. For the rest of the day, I could not shake the sick ball which tumbled in my stomach whenever I recalled the image of the girl on the green.

I DIDN'T SEE her again until the next day.

I had spent that morning with Miss Grey, sorting though some papers and preparing the menu for Cook. Miss Grey liked to think of herself as someone with purpose. She enjoyed long mornings surrounded by papers of her accounts, though they never told her anything new. She had a private bookkeeper, whom I had never had the pleasure of meeting, and occasionally he sent records her way so she could frown over how much Cook had spent on partridges or fresh fish, or how much lace cost nowadays, or how she would soon have to be darning her own stockings. I tried not to remind her that I already darned her stockings.

Miss Grey was a miser, you see. She was also a hypochondriac, though I hadn't known that when I applied for the role as her companion several months previously. She had indeed seemed the epitome of ill health when I had visited one bleak November day, the rain blowing inland in horizontal sheets from the English Channel. She had been sitting in her drawing room, the fire stacked high, the flames grasping at her skirts. She had pressed a handkerchief to her reddened nose for the entire meeting whilst I had poured tea and cooed over her and nodded in sympathy as she described just how ill she was. And I had believed her, for her lungs really did rasp whenever she took a breath, and her hand really did shake when she brought her teacup to her lips. So I had accepted the position as her companion, a paid friend, thinking she must have been somewhere near death.

A mild case of the influenza, her grave illness turned out to be. The snivels dried up within a week of my arrival, and though she held her face over bowls of steaming water until spring came, her lungs had cleared of their sickness before Christmas.

Now the summer was here, she was forever in fear of the typhus or cholera. She ordered me to eat a little of her food before she ate it herself and to keep the windows closed if the wind blew in such a direction as to bring the hot, foul smells of the town our way. She would insist on taking the carriage out into the countryside most days; it was the only place where she felt she could breathe properly.

But in the mornings, we stayed inside surrounded by dusty papers, filling endless minutes with endless drivel, until she handed me the much-deliberated menu, which was usually the same food she had ordered the day before, and I escaped to the basement.

Cook was a large woman with an unhappy countenance that I believed would have soured the milk had she looked at it for too long. She sweated even in the winter and constantly wiped her forehead on her apron so that the yellowed tip of it often had to be bleached. She didn't like me at first because of the way I turned my nose up at the food she cooked, for after all, I was sure some of her sweat must have fallen into it. But after I had caught her helping herself to the larder's contents and had consciously turned my head, she came to grudgingly accept me. We usually grunted at each other and said goodnight when she left after dinner to go back to her family in the town. Miss Grey didn't like servants in the house, so she said. She thought them dirty and that their dirt would permeate into the upper quarters of the house, especially at night, and weaken her. It was also rather handy that she didn't like too many staff, for her accounts couldn't take it, so I discovered, again, too late.

Miss Grey lived off an allowance, once given to her by her father, now by her brother. Meagre was not the word. Whilst Mr Grey languished in his London mansion, his sister had to make do with one cook and one companion, and I acted more as a lady's maid and housekeeper than as one of my station should have been accustomed to living.

And so it was, the following day, after I had emptied her pot, after I had brought her breakfast crockery down to wash, after I had wet the fly papers in the scullery and had hung them in the kitchens, that I saw from the window a white skirt. The kitchens being in the basement, I could only see the very bottom of Luella's dress and her worn, black boots. I thought her feet must have been very hot, for I myself was sticky; the wind had disappeared that day and the air was close. I collected the piles of flies' bodies from the kitchen floor in some old newspaper, took them outside and threw them in the hedgerow beside the house, then tiptoed up the side passage and came out in front of the kitchen window.

She stood above me, looking down on me, silent. I climbed the short flight of steps and came level with her. Both of us were in the shade of a laburnum tree whose golden flowers had been shed a few weeks ago, and now the sun only dappled through its leaves. The green in front of the house was quiet at that time – midday, too hot for ladies in petticoats and corsets. The air was lazy all about us as we stared at each other, wondering who would speak first.

Now that I was there with her, I didn't know what to say. Up close, I could make out the smattering of freckles over her skin, and the longer I looked, the more I thought I recognised her features – the pointedness of the tip of her nose, the prominent bow in her upper lip, the faint crease between her brows. I was about to remember something, then she spoke and the familiarity of her vanished.

'Bonnie Hearn?' she said. Her voice seemed to startle her; it was loud in the stillness of the day. She cleared her throat and her hand rose to her chest. It was then that I noticed the chain about her neck, though whatever was on the end of it was hidden underneath her bodice. She wound the chain around her finger once, then dropped her hand as if it had pinched her and waited for my response.

'Who are you?' I said.

She met my gaze, and there was a hardness in her face. She seemed determined, suddenly, and though her voice was quieter when she spoke again, her words were clear.

'Meet me in the tea room on Giles Street tomorrow at three.'

Her accent was pronounced, familiar, the sound of this part of the country. I tried again to think where I might have seen her before, but she remained a mystery. Even so, it was obvious she knew me.

'I can't. I am afraid I am busy –'

'I know Miss Grey likes to sleep then, and I know how you fills your time when she does so.'

If I'd been anyone else, or if she hadn't been so young and

such a small country girl, I would have blushed. Instead I smiled, almost laughed. What a preposterous predicament!

'All right,' I said, for now my curiosity was piqued. It could have been a lucky guess; she might not have known what I really did when Miss Grey slept, but if she did, I wondered how long she had been watching me. The amusement I had been feeling quickly vanished.

She nodded once, then turned. Her boots clicked on the pavement and echoed as she walked away from me, the vision of her simmering under the heat of the sun.

I HAD NEVER BEEN to the tea room on Giles Street before. Like most of Stowmouth's buildings, this one was rather crooked, and the top of my hat caught on the door frame as I entered. It had a smell to it: stale tea and sweet cakes left out in the heat. Dozy flies wavered in the air above middle-class ladies' heads, and I wondered why they hadn't hung themselves some fly papers as I made my way to a small table in the corner of the cramped room, my skirts banging against the closely packed tables. After squeezing into a chair, which faced the door so that I could see Luella clearly when she arrived, and after dragging my feet off the sticky floor and placing them on the table legs, I smiled and nodded at the women about me. I ordered tea for two.

I had arrived at the tea room promptly, of course, and waited happily for the first five minutes, filling the time by watching the steam pouring out of the teapot spout. Yet as time lengthened, I became agitated. A couple of the women finished their tea and left, nodding at me as they went, and the others who remained looked at me and gossiped to each other; no doubt, I was the latest topic of conversation.

I removed my lace gloves and poured the tea which was, by that point, half cold and as dark as molasses. I sipped the drink and winced at the strength of it, then put the cup into its saucer gently and smiled at the women. They blushed to know I had caught them gawping.

Five and twenty minutes had passed, and I was fastening on my gloves and readying myself to depart, chastising my own foolishness, when the tea room door squeaked open and Luella entered. She was too short to hit her head on the door frame, but she stopped just inside the room and stared about her. Perhaps the afternoon sun had made her blind and her eyes needed to adjust to the dimness. Perhaps she was not quite in her right mind. Either way, she was caught off guard for a few moments, and I was able to study her quickly and collect myself. I patted down my skirt, eased off my gloves and laid them on my lap, and arranged my face so that the frown had disappeared by the time she looked at me.

Her arrival had caused something of a stir. The two tables of women stared at her blatantly; the middle classes could sniff out a working-class girl a mile off. But Luella seemed not to notice, or at least she did not care. She slipped between the tables easily with her narrow skirt and sat on the chair opposite me without saying a word. I had risen to greet her, but I sat down again when it was clear we were not there to be polite with each other.

She unlaced the bow under her jaw and pulled off her bonnet. Her hair was gold and red, though it frizzed at the scalp in an ugly manner – I supposed that was due to the heat. She scratched at her parting with her gloveless fingernails and sighed. She never looked at me, but instead her gaze flitted around the items on the table, and her tongue pushed against her upper lip.

'Could we have some more tea, please?' I said to the waitress behind the counter, and I smiled again at the women who stared at me and my odd companion. I let the smile fall on Luella as I said between my teeth, 'You are late.'

She nodded distractedly, and her hand dropped from her parting and clutched at the chain about her neck. I waited for her to speak – for after all, it was she who had arranged this meeting – but she remained silent even after the waitress had set another pot of tea and another clean cup and saucer on our table. I poured the blissfully weak tea into our two cups, dropped a cube of sugar into hers because she looked like she needed it, then pushed it in her direction. She took it, and I saw that her hands were slightly cracked and a little rough in the creases of the knuckle, not soft and white like my own despite the chores Miss Grey had me do too often.

I let her drink before I said, 'I have fifteen minutes before I must return. What do you want from me?'

My comment did not hasten her. She drank again, and with each gulp, she seemed to grow calmer until another five minutes had passed and there was nothing in her cup but some undissolved grains of sugar. She put the cup in its saucer, and finally her blue eyes looked up at me.

'You don't remember me,' she said.

I shook my head; I would not admit she seemed familiar.

'You knew my father.'

'Did I? Who is he?'

'Were.'

'Sorry?'

She wet her lips. 'Your question should have been, who were he?'

She was intense for such a small thing. She reminded me of a ferret as it claws down a rabbit hole, and I didn't like the feel of it.

'Who was he?'

'Samuel Blyth.'

The name rolled over my mind like waves over the ocean. It had been a long time since I'd heard it. How long? I tried to think. How many years had passed; how many Christmases had I seen; how many ladies had I been companion to since then?

She saw me frowning, and a glimmer of triumph shone in her face. Then I realised it was Samuel whom I had seen in her yesterday; it was Samuel's turn of the nose and full lip that I had recognised in her dainty features.

I thought of the child I had seen with Samuel all those years ago, running circles around him as they walked up the long, cobbled path, the dust from another hot summer swirling about them. She had been a plain girl back then. Her hair had been copper, not as light as now, and she had been plump in the limbs and cheeks. I remembered Samuel shooing her away from him so she would go and see Mrs Campbell inside the house. I remembered her running for the back door, straight past me, smiling and showing her teeth as she bounded into the kitchen whilst I waited for her father.

'Luella,' she said, and startled me out of my thoughts. 'My name is Luella.'

How could I have forgotten? I had never heard that name before I went to Mrs Campbell's and had never heard it since. I thought it too pretty for a girl like her back then. Now I saw she had grown into it, and for a moment, I wondered if she had actually been born on a Monday, for she certainly wasn't fair as a child. Perhaps she was Wednesday's child, considering what happened.

'What do you want, Luella?'

She leaned back in her chair. I took the time to study her dress more closely. It had tight patterns of faded yellow flowers on the white cotton, and parts of it were thinner and more frayed than others; it was nothing like the finer dresses she used to wear.

'A name.'

I laughed. It was an ominous meeting for something so simple as a name.

'The name of the man you worked with at Mrs Campbell's.'

'You will have to be more specific.'

'You only worked with him and my pa. I know my pa's name. What's the other man's name?'

Somehow I managed not to stumble. I thought ignorance would be the best tactic. 'How should I know?'

'His first name were Frank. You knew him.'

'Did I?' The laugh broke out of me again. 'You know more about me than I know about myself.'

'He looked after the horses and the gardens for Mrs Campbell. And Bonnie' – the way she said my name made me shiver – 'don't patronise me. Tell me his name.'

The smile dropped from my face. 'I cannot remember him.'

'Tall, he was, at least I thought him tall, but I suppose I were just a child then. He had hair to his shoulders – I remember that. It looked dirty and greasy. He were quiet too; I never heard him speak much.'

I shook my head, and she sighed disappointedly. I thought she might have accepted my forgetfulness, nodded, and thanked me for my time. I did not know her well at all.

'You'll tell me his name, Bonnie, or I'll tell Miss Grey about the trinkets what you've been stealing from her.'

So it was not a lucky guess. The heat in the room vanished. I must have flinched, for she continued unperturbed: 'I only need his name.'

I cleared my throat. 'How did you find me?'

She smiled and showed her teeth like she used to do, though the smile didn't touch her eyes. 'I remembered you, and your name, and I went round asking. You went to Mrs

Massey after Mrs Campbell, then Mrs Davey, then Miss Hall, then Mrs King, and now Miss Grey.'

Again, I shivered. 'You really do know me well.'

'You have what I want.'

I raised my brows. 'You did all that searching, just for a name?'

'Yes.'

'And you have been watching me?'

'For a while.' She scratched her parting again, and flakes of skin fluttered from her scalp. 'It don't matter to me what you take from Miss Grey; she's a stranger to me.'

'Why bring it up then?'

'Leverage. I need that name. Give it me, and you'll never see me again. Don't, and I'll go to Grey or the police. I ain't bothered about which.'

My lips felt tight. I did not want to give her the name, for I thought that as soon as I did, something terrible would begin. But neither did I want to be found out for a thief, and I had no doubt that she would be true to her word.

It was only a name, after all.

'Adams, I think it was. Frank Adams. But it was a long time ago; I might have remembered it wrong.'

She pushed out her chair, rose from her seat, and fastened her bonnet. The air of madness had evaporated from her; she was sedate, calm, and even more disturbing. 'Thank you for your help.'

She turned to walk away, and I stood to stop her. My crinoline caught the edge of the table and made the cups and saucers rattle. Everyone in the tea room faced me, and so I patted my skirt and waited for them to lose interest as Luella craned her neck to listen to what I had to say.

'I can't be sure that was his name.'

'I think it were; it sounds familiar to me now you've said it.'

'Why do you want it?'

'I'm going to find him.'

'What? Why? He could be anywhere.'

She shrugged. 'I'll find him.'

It was a ridiculous notion. She could never possibly be successful, but still I asked, 'How?'

'The same way I found you.'

I tried to laugh at her confidence, but it was her confidence which was so unnerving. 'That could take forever.'

'Then I will look for him forever.'

'And if you do find him' – I lowered my voice so the women, who were being too quiet, could not hear – 'what will you do?'

'I will kill him.'

HER ANSWER HAD STUNNED ME. I found myself staring at the space she had been standing in for ages after she had gone. The waitress coughed and startled me; I hadn't seen her come so close. She was a middle-aged woman, unused to smiling, and she stared pointedly at my purse. I found her the coins she required and stumbled out of that horrid, poky place, casting over a chair with my skirt as I went.

Outside, I breathed the cooler air and closed my eyes against the glare of the sun. I should have brought a parasol with me. I raised my hand to bring my eyes into shade and searched Giles Street for a sign of Luella. I was too late; I had stood too long in the tea room. There were no peculiar girls with white dresses milling around.

I tried to recall the time on the tea room clock; it must have been nearly four. I needed to return to Miss Grey soon to be there to wake her, for she complained of headaches if she slept too long in the afternoons. I swivelled to my right, resolved to head back to the house, but my feet would not move in that direction.

I needed to find Luella.

I strode deeper into Stowmouth. I had never liked the seaside town. It seemed like it was trying to be something it was not. New hotels had been built along the seafront, their whitewashed faces gaping out at the water, their new windows gleaming in the sunlight, turning their backs on the Elizabethan town in distaste. There was a mixture of people in this place which was once nothing but a small fishing port where many a smuggler's ship had been wrecked on the rocks beneath the waves. It was possible to tell the people whose ancestors had lived here, for they had a certain look: stocky and broad and weathered, always ready with a mean glare for any newcomer. The newcomers were those who thought the sea air would cure them like Miss Grey. They lived in the newly built houses on the edges of the town or took long residences in the hotels. And then there were the people who worked in the cities and used the railroads to take them for days out with their children who swamped the pavements and dug holes in the sand for unsuspecting victims to fall into.

It was these kinds of people who littered the scene before me now. Low- to middle-class families, the women wearing dresses from a decade ago but shaped around a crinoline, the men who had acquired walking canes and bowler hats though they had no need of them, the children who demanded items out of shop windows as if it were their right to have them. They ambled down the narrow streets and blocked my view of any girl in white. I swerved them all, leaving them in clouds of perfume and dust as I marched past, panicking that I had lost Luella forever.

Then I rounded a corner, and a white flash as bright as a shard of glass glinting in the sun caught my eye. I grabbed my skirts and walked as fast as I could until my armpits grew damp and my chemise stuck to my back. Men parted for me, ogling me as I broke into a trot to reach her.

'Luella!'

She stopped by a grocer's shop and turned to smile at me. I was panting by this point and finding it hard to fill my lungs. I rested my hands on my knees for a second and gulped in the air.

'Are you all right, Bonnie? You want to sit?'

I shook my head and straightened. My cheeks were throbbing – I dared not think how red they must have been – and I retrieved a handkerchief from my bag and wiped my brow underneath my hat. She was still smiling at me, laughing at me, I thought.

'What do you mean, you'll kill him?'

'What I said.'

'Why?'

'Because my pa were innocent. Because Frank Adams did something evil, and I won't let him get away with it no longer.'

'No.' I licked my dry lips. 'No, Luella, you are wrong.'

'What do you mean? You saying my pa were guilty?'

Guilty. The word echoed in my mind. 'No. Perhaps. I don't know.'

'Say my pa were guilty again and I'll go to the police right now and tell them about your thieving!'

I couldn't speak for a moment. I did not know what to say or how I might be able to reason with her. I needed time to think.

'All right ... sorry. Where are you staying?' I said as I tried to slow my breathing.

She looked at the window above the grocer's shop. 'Why?'

'When will you start looking for ... Frank?'

'I'll leave tomorrow, first thing. Don't worry, Bonnie.' She went to touch my arm, but her fingers wavered an inch from me before she put her hand by her side again. 'I won't bother you again.'

'You kill him, Luella, and they'll hang you.'

She looked me straight in the eye. 'I don't care.'

'Please, Luella. You are so young.' How old must she have been? Certainly no more than twenty. 'You have your own life you must live.'

She kicked a box of cabbages in front of the grocer's shop, and the green globes shook and wobbled like so many chopped-off heads. 'You don't know anything, Bonnie.'

We were causing a scene; the grocer inside was looking at us through the window, and the delivery boy, who had an armful of vegetables, was watching us as he placed his produce in his basket.

'Please.' I took her by the elbow and brought her closer to me so she would hear my whisper. 'Please just stay here for a few days and think about what you are doing. Perhaps we could meet for tea again? I should like to know about you, what you have been doing since ...' I was saying all the wrong things in my panic. I pinched the bridge of my nose and took a deep breath. 'Just wait while I think things through.'

'This has nothing to do with you, Bonnie. You don't need to think about me or my father or Frank Adams ever again.'

'I do,' I sighed. I would scare her off if I was not careful. 'I will not stop you going after him, if only you will wait for two more days.'

'Why?'

'Because ...' What was I doing? I was so desperate for an end to this bizarre meeting. If only I had never agreed to see her! But I had, and now I was stuck with her and the notion that she intended to murder someone. I could not let her leave Stowmouth and carry out her plan, and so I promised, 'I will help you find him if you will let me.'

I HAD TO GO THEN, for the church clock struck four. I strode away, checking over my shoulder every few seconds to see if she was still there, still watching me. She was. I hesitated on the corner of the street and looked at her again. If only I could have glued her to the spot! I had no conviction that she would wait for me, but just before I walked on, she nodded, and I could do nothing but hope she would still be in Stowmouth in the morning.

MISS GREY WAS foul with me when I returned. She had dreamt of disease, had woken in a frenzy, sweating and screaming, and Cook had seen to her.

'Filthy woman,' Miss Grey said, as I was helping her into her chair in the drawing room. 'No wonder I am so ill. Write to my brother and tell him I will need a new cook by next week.'

'Can I make you some tea?'

She was scowling at the light from the window. 'Shut those curtains.'

Below, with the heat from the sun finally abating for the day, women had returned to parade about the green. I scanned the view as I clutched the heavy silk curtains, my eyes resting on the mass of grey and white buildings, trying to pinpoint the location of the grocer's shop. Luella was there somewhere, brooding no doubt.

How would she know where to look for Frank? Where would she start? It was an absurd notion, and I told myself that there was no way she could possibly find him no matter how long she searched. But then, I reminded myself, she had found me.

'Are you sick?' Miss Grey said.

I turned and found her cowering against the light, her eyes wide as she stared worriedly at me.

'No.' I drew the curtains and plunged the room into darkness.

'That's better.' Miss Grey rested her head against the back of her chair whilst I lit the oil lamp and sat in the seat opposite her. A book was on the table beside me, and I found the page I had finished yesterday and began to read aloud. It was not long before Miss Grey's mouth fell slack and revealed her grey tongue. Everything about the woman was grey, as though she would not allow the glow of life to penetrate her.

I set the book on the table and listened to her heavy breathing. I was picking my lips before I knew what I was doing, making them bleed before I could stop myself. Mother used to smack me whenever she saw me do it, for it showed me to be worried or upset, and I was never allowed to be either of those things. I shoved my hands under my legs to keep myself still.

Why should I have been so scared by this girl, anyway? I tried to shrug my fears away, casting them and Luella off as ridiculous. Luella could search all she liked for Frank. She could even find him; there was nothing to say she would be able to kill him. Thinking and doing were very different things.

I closed my eyes. The air was hot and was pressing down on me as it had been in the tea room on Giles Street. I unfastened the buttons at my neck and felt sweat trickle onto my collarbone.

I was underestimating Luella, and I knew it.

Silently, I left Miss Grey in the drawing room and descended to the morning room where she kept her papers.

The air was lighter in here, for I had opened the window earlier, and a pleasant breeze blew into the space. I sat at her desk, took a sheet of thick, waxy paper, and dabbed the pen into the ink pot.

Mr Grey,

I am writing on behalf of your sister. Miss Grey requests a new cook, for she is displeased with the current woman who has the position and fears the food is making her ill.

She will also need a new companion, for my own aunt has become gravely ill, and I must leave to care for her. She has no other family besides myself.

My deepest apologies,

Bonnie Hearn

I sealed the letter, then took another piece of paper. My hand shook, and ink spotted the page. I hoped he would be able to understand my slanted letters.

Frank,

Luella Blyth wants you dead. She is hunting you. I said I would help only so I may know her intentions. There is something about her. She is a danger – to us both. How should I proceed?

Burn this.

Yours,

B

CHAPTER 2

The following day passed in agony as I waited for Frank's response. And then the next morning Miss Grey insisted on the carriage ride, though I warned of rain clouds building on the horizon. I was right, for halfway through our journey the heavens opened. Miss Grey complained of the noise on the carriage roof and held her head in her hands, whimpering in pain. The windows had to be closed so she would not be splashed by the water, and I shall never know how I managed to contain myself for the remaining twenty minutes of the ride as the air grew thick and her whining grew louder.

At least the onset of a headache sent her straight to bed when we returned. I stroked her hair as she closed her eyes and hummed some word-less tune that my mother once hummed to me until she fell asleep.

Then I was out the door.

The rain was beginning to ease off, as summer rain does. Only a few fat spots hit my hat and made black circles on my pale blue gown. The air was sweet – that delicious scent of dry earth once it's been quenched – and I found that the freshness allowed me a moment of calm.

Nevertheless, I was expecting Luella to have disappeared when I arrived at the grocer's shop. The owner showed me the stairs at the rear of the building and said it was the first door on the left. I knocked, my breath held, readying myself for no reply when the doorknob rattled.

'Come in,' Luella said, half hidden behind the frame as if she'd been expecting me. Perhaps she had been watching from her window.

I stepped inside. The place was neat; the bed was made, the surfaces clear. A little bag lay beside one flat pillow – Luella's things packed and ready to go.

'I did not know if you would still be here.'

'You said you'd help me.' She wandered to the table in front of the open window, sat on one of the two chairs, then nodded for me to take the other.

The bare floorboards creaked as I crept towards her. What must the grocer have been thinking downstairs, for it was surely strange to have two women, so different in appearance and station, meet covertly in a rented room?

'Are you too warm?' she said.

I shook my head, peeled off my gloves, and pressed a cool hand to my hot cheek. From the street below, I heard short snippets of conversations, women laughing, children's shoes beating on the kerbsides, and I had a quick moment of dread. I would be leaving this place soon, and though I hated it most of the time, I suddenly realised I would miss it. The thought surprised me; my own tenderness towards places always surprised me for I had never lived anywhere longer than two years. Stowmouth's peculiar ways had grown on me, though I had never admitted it to myself until then.

'How are you going to help me?' She had crossed her

arms and was leaning back in her chair as if my answer might be a piece of entertainment to be enjoyed.

I breathed in deeply. 'I know him. Frank, I mean.'

There was no hint of surprise on her face other than the raising of one eyebrow. She really was very pretty, in a young and vulnerable sort of way. The more I looked at her, the more I was drawn to her. I was watching her pretty lips when she said, 'How?'

'I … We …' The words stuck. I let out my frustration in a sigh and tugged the chain which hung around my neck out from under my gown. A plain gold band dangled from the end of it. She gazed at it like it was a hypnotist's pendulum.

'Married?'

I nodded, then slipped the ring back into its place. She was frowning as I looked at her again.

'It's easier for me to find work as a single woman,' I said.

She sniffed, and her face became smooth, resigned. She stared through the open window, and a film of tears smudged her eyes. 'Are you here to plead for him?'

'For Frank, but for you too, Luella.' I reached across the table and took her hands. They were shockingly cold, and she held still as I touched her. 'Whatever Frank has done, it cannot be undone.'

She withdrew her hands from mine. 'Whatever he has done? You know what he's done?'

'I can imagine what you think he has done.'

'And what's that? Go on, tell me. Tell me, Bonnie!'

'You think he killed Mr Campbell. You think he set your father up to hang for a crime that was not his.'

Her lips parted, and it seemed like she was having trouble breathing. 'Did he? Is that the truth?'

I stood from my chair and paced the floor; I could not look out of the window at the happy families whose day was passing just like any other day.

'Bonnie?'

I waved my gloves before my heated face. Everywhere was so warm!

'Bonnie, is Frank a murderer?'

I couldn't get my words out.

'Bonnie, tell me! Am I right?'

'Yes!' I threw the gloves on the bed, then sank onto the thin mattress with my back to her; I could not meet her gaze. 'Yes, you are right, Luella.'

I heard her breath escape from her mouth, then a faint sniffing as she sobbed. Her face was in her hands, her shoulders quivering. I reached out to comfort her, but when I touched her, she leapt from her seat. She marched towards the door and turned the key – she was locking me in! She took the key out and dangled it before her.

'You will tell me where he is.' She dropped the key down the front of her gown.

'Luella, he is a dangerous man.'

'Tell me, Bonnie.'

I edged closer to her, hands up, as if I was approaching a wild beast. 'Luella, he is a violent man. He has hurt me. You think he will have any concerns about hurting you?'

'I will hurt him.'

'How?'

'I will beat him.'

I would have laughed if I had not been so scared; she was talking nonsense.

'He will kill you in an instant if he suspects you. He will kill you before you can lay one finger on him.'

'I will kill him!' Her scream smashed into a cry. She doubled over, but I reached her before she fell to the floor and guided her to sit on the bed. I held her close to me, despite the throbbing heat that was coming from her, and let her weep against my bosom.

'How can you stand it?' she whispered once she had drained herself of emotion. 'How can you bear to know what you know and live with it?'

'I have no choice. I married him before I knew what he was.'

'A murderer, you mean?'

'Yes,' I whispered, and a finger of heat scratched down my spine.

'You could be free of him.' She said the words quietly. 'Do you love him?'

'Not anymore.'

She raised her head and looked up at me through her wet lashes, and for a moment I imagined her as my own daughter and rubbed her back and smiled kindly at her.

'Then let us kill him,' she said.

'Us?'

'I will do it, but you must tell me how. You know him, you know what will make him suspicious.' She took my hands this time, and again I flinched at the iciness of her skin. 'Please, Bonnie. For my father's sake. For mine. For your sake.'

'I do not think I can. He is a smart man; he will know something is wrong.'

'Only if you show it.' Luella unravelled herself from my embrace. Her face had paled from its redness, and now only the apples of her cheeks remained flushed and her eyes glassy from crying. She led me off the bed and to the table and chairs and made me sit. I let the breeze from the open window wash over me as she spoke. 'Smart, you say. But I think men tend to lose that smartness with a woman, don't they? I think they quite forget just how dangerous we can be.'

A sickness was building in my stomach. I swallowed it down, but still my insides rolled around. I pushed my arms against my bodice and sat up straight. 'You are not strong enough to beat him to death, Luella. That man has taken more fights than a tomcat.'

'What about when he's sleeping?'

I tasted the tang of blood on my tongue and realised I'd been biting my lip. 'What do you plan to do once you've killed him?'

She sighed, shrugged.

'I will not hang for you, Luella.'

She turned her head towards me, ever so slowly, and gave me the coldest look I had ever seen in my life. 'I know.'

After glaring at me for a moment, she dragged her eyes off me to examine the patterns in the wood of the table. Her hand flew to her chest, and she fiddled with the chain.

'Have you any money?' I asked, trying to keep the tremor out of my voice.

'A little.'

'Enough for a boat?'

'I don't know.'

My fear was turning to frustration. She was closing in on herself; I could see her eyes hardening, and I wondered what thoughts were playing through her mind. I could not let too many memories surface for her, and I was getting impatient for the meeting to be over, for things to be sorted.

There was no use trying to change her mind or steer her in the direction I wanted her to take. She was not going to give up; I could see it in the set of her lips, a determination which had been mirrored in her father. But I would not think of Samuel now. I could not let my conscience be pricked.

'Arsenic.'

She raised her eyes to me. 'What?'

'Kill Frank with arsenic.'

'How?'

'Fly papers.' I had been mulling the idea over all morning.

All those little flies on the kitchen floor, dead before they knew it. It was not a quick death, nor painless, and for that I was sorry. 'It will not be as obvious as a blow to the head. By the time the body is found, we can be halfway across the ocean.'

'You'll come with me?'

'I shall have to, won't I?'

'Why?'

'To make sure you keep our secret.' I smiled, though it was a strain. 'I shall lead you to Frank. I shall ready the poison. I shall keep him oblivious to our plan. And then you may pour him some tea and watch him drink it. Watch him die.'

I could feel her buzz, her energy, chafing as she imagined it. The tiniest of smiles spread to a wide grin, and then she laughed. It was not the kind of laugh one would expect to roar from such a girl; it was manic and made me edge away from her. She wiped the corners of her eyes as she collected herself, blew out her breath, and shook her head.

'You really are something, Bonnie.'

'Will you do it, or will you leave now? It is not too late. It is easy to play at being murderers, but best for our fantasies to stay as fantasies.'

'This ain't no fantasy.' She was serious again, and her unpredictability was something that made me wary of her. 'My pa is dead. I will have justice.' She walked to the door, dipped her hand into her bodice, and produced the key. She opened the door and ushered me out.

'We leave at dawn,' she said.

I nodded before scurrying away. Back in my chamber, I lit a fire in the grate. I took Frank's note from under my pillow where I had hidden it earlier and read it one last time before throwing it on the flames.

Bonnie,

Bring her to me. Keep her as your friend and go along with her plans. Prepare yourself and what we will need to end this once and for all.

Frank

AFTER COOK LEFT for the evening, I sat with Miss Grey in the drawing room and drank sherry with her. My clothes were already packed in my case, the trinkets I had stolen wrapped safely inside my skirts. All I had to do was wait, but I had never been very good at that.

'Stop it,' Miss Grey said, pointing at my leg which was tapping, though I hadn't been aware of it. I held myself still and gazed out of the window.

The sky was streaked in pinks and oranges, like stretched lily petals, and gulls glided across it, calling out to each other before they went to sleep for the night.

I ran my fingers over the silk of the chair arm, felt the lumps of the stuffing under my legs, pressed my feet into the thick carpet. I smiled at Miss Grey, and she smiled back, and I brought my sherry glass to my mouth to feel the shapes of the cut glass against my lips.

Odd, how we want to drink everything in when we are about to lose it all. I wished to print that night on my eyelids, to store it in my memory forever. Not because I would mourn the loss of Miss Grey or her house, but because it had been a part of me, another small piece that made me a whole, another bit of me that must be lost.

I had been the same when I had left my mother, and I had promised myself I would not forget that night, but over the years it had faded so that I could not be sure if the rug before the fire had been patterned or plain, or if we had eaten meat pie, or if I really had downed my glass of beer before I told mother I loved her, or if her husband had opened my door that night. I could not be sure of the memory at all and wondered if I had imagined those few final hours, when I still called myself a daughter, so that they seemed more special than they really were.

It would be the same with this night and with Miss Grey. In a few years' time, I would forget how the chair creaked with every breath I took, how the sherry stung my sore lip, how the waves of the sea less than a mile away acted as a constant lullaby in the background of our lives.

'I have some grave news, Miss Grey.' She had become sleepy; I had left it until now to tell her, when her strength had ebbed for the day. 'My aunt is unwell.'

Miss Grey's eyelids strained to open. 'What is wrong?'

'Something in her stomach and bowels; I should not like to tell you the details. She is in great pain.'

Miss Grey grunted, and her eyelids drooped. She never had sympathy for anyone, for she never believed anyone was worse off than herself. It made me flare to see her so careless, for what if I really did have an aunt who was dying in such a horrid way? What if I really was on the brink of losing someone I loved, and the only thing she could do was grunt?

'So I shall be leaving you. Tomorrow.'

Her eyes flew open, and she stammered for a reply. I had risen by that point, and I was shaking out my skirts and straightening the chair when she grabbed my hand.

'You cannot leave me.'

'Your brother knows of my situation. He shall find someone else for you. You must understand, Miss Grey, I have no choice but to return to my aunt and care for her.'

'You must care for me!' Her anger was breaking into fear. She started to cry. I kneeled before her and took her hands.

'You have been so very kind to me, Miss Grey. Truly, I wish to stay here with you, but my aunt is the only family I have left. You understand?'

She was sobbing, and her mucus dripped onto my skin.

'Someone else must be able to care for her. Why should you go? Why should you leave me?'

'It is my duty.' I peeled my hands out of her grasp, and she cried as if she was a babe torn from the teat. 'Mr Grey will have everything arranged, I am sure. You will not be alone for long. Now, let's get you into bed.'

I guided her to her chamber, dressed her in her night-gown, and set her under her covers. I rubbed her cold feet with my hands, filled a bed pan with hot coals from the grate and put it in with her. I perched on the mattress and stroked her hair, which was long and grey and as coarse as hemp.

'Will you sing?' she asked, clutching her covers to her chin.

I hummed the tune for her and brushed away an old tear that lay on her cheek and stayed with her until she slept. Then I tiptoed to the morning room and unlocked the bureau. I found the little box at the back where she kept her money and which she opened once a month to check there was still the same amount in there as the month before. I took five pounds. By the time she counted it again, she would have a new companion and, as such, a suspect. How Miss Grey would lament the loss of her old, trusted friend, Bonnie Hearn!

DOWNSTAIRS IN THE BASEMENT, I soaked the fly papers and sat on the kitchen stool, chin resting in my hand as I listened to the night-time noises of the house. The world around me was cooling, the stars were twinkling, and the moon was shining over Stowmouth. Somewhere in the mire of the streets, people would be as awake as I was, doing goodness knows what under cover of darkness. I thought of Luella amidst the thieves and whores, and I wondered if she too was sitting on a chair at the table and gazing out of the window, thinking about what I was doing. Perhaps she was in bed, sleeping soundly, content in the knowledge that her plan was about to commence. I would never know how she spent that night.

In the flickering candlelight, I poured the fly-paper water into a flask. It would pass as whiskey if anyone asked. I pressed the papers into the range so Cook would burn them in the morning.

Upstairs in my quaint little room at the side of the house which had a partial view of the green (Miss Grey had the chamber at the back of the house overlooking her garden which she liked to watch but never venture into), I sat on the bed and gazed at the sky. It was navy and seemed to glisten like velvet; it was a beautiful night to commence a terrible thing – wasn't it always the same? The note to Frank rested in my hands.

Frank,

We are on our way. I have the poison. Be ready.

B

I stared at those words over and over again, trying to decide if part of me felt any guilt. Was there a stirring in my gut? Did my eyes prick with tears? No.

I must say that I was not a completely callous woman. Hadn't I tried to dissuade her, to tell her that Frank was a dangerous man, that death lay ahead of her? And hadn't she relished the challenge?

I thought of her looking up at me through her lashes after she had cried on my shoulder. I imagined her as my own child, and still nothing changed in my heart. She was not a child. She was not someone to be cuddled and petted. She was a threat, and she was here for blood. If she baited the bear, she would be bitten. She just didn't know it was me she was baiting.

The sun's pale rays swept across the sky and drowned the stars. I shut the door gently, lifted my heels as I stepped out into the yard, and made my way up the basement steps.

Once on the green, I took a moment to look back at Miss Grey's house. The white of it glowed in the dawn and made the windows appear blacker than ever. I imagined myself in the top window, bending over to dust the sill and dropping the silver button box into my apron pocket as Luella had seen me do. How many times had she watched me before that day? Now, as I looked at the house, I realised I had been like an animal in a zoo. I turned my back on it so I would not have to worry about what other secrets I had given away.

The town was coming alive with the dawn chorus. Boats were already on the sea, and the costermongers were calling out their deals for the day. I waited on the street corner and watched the grocer's shop. The man was stumbling around behind the window, rubbing his eyes and yawning as he wiped down the counter.

Luella's window was open, as it had been yesterday, and there was a faint yellow glow in the room from her candle. So she had not yet left, and she was not watching.

I hurried to the post office a few doors down from the grocer's and slipped the note for Frank through the letter box. I closed my eyes and prayed to God that it reached him before we did, though I had little faith that God would listen, for it had been years since I'd last spoken to Him.

I was walking towards the grocer's when I had the sensation of someone beside me.

'Good morning.'

It was all I could do to hold the scream inside my mouth. To my right, Luella grinned wildly. Gripping my arm, she marched us through Stowmouth, her bag battering against my thighs as my own leather case hung heavy in my hand. I was gasping by the time she let us slow down. She had walked us out of the town, off the road, and to the banks of the river.

'What on earth?'

'We have to hurry before the day gets too hot,' she said. 'Follow the river.' She was making little sense; she was crazed again.

'We should find a cart going to Exeter. Come, we are going the wrong way.'

'Why Exeter?'

'To get a train.'

'No trains.' She shook her head and stamped her foot.

'How do you suppose we reach him then?'

'Walk.'

My laughter echoed in the valley.

'It ain't that far,' she said.

My laugh stopped. She pinched her lips.

'How do you know how far it is?' I said.

She kicked a clump of grass free with her toe and shrugged. 'I guessed you wouldn't live too far from your husband. Am I right?'

She was right, but that didn't quieten my unease. 'It is far enough to warrant a train.'

'No trains.' She shook her head so much that her cheeks wobbled. 'I won't go on a train.'

She was a silly country girl, wasn't she? Scared of anything new. Perhaps she thought her head would fly off or her lungs would be crushed from the speed of it. And there was no point in protesting, for really, it was better this way. Frank would have more time; I would have more time. But the thought of walking all those miles made my feet hurt before we had begun.

'A stagecoach,' she said.

When was the last time she had left her hometown? 'Hardly any operate nowadays.'

‘There’s some still going. We’ll use them or walk.’

I sighed. ‘Fine. But I will not wear out these shoes for you.’

She nodded, and the madness again slid off her. I led the way out of the valley and over the wet grass until we reached the north road. I stopped and listened for the sound of wheels, but the air was filled only with birds which sang to the glory of a new day.

I turned northwards and glared at the hill before me. ‘This way.’

CHAPTER 3

A coach did not come. A cart did not come. For a while, I had the awful notion that I was directing us out of our way, but then a marker told us we were five miles from Honiton, and I could breathe again.

The road was hard under my feet. My shoes were not meant for walking; the leather was too soft, the heel too high. There were blisters forming, and I could feel the pressure of them building at the back of my ankles and on the balls of my feet. Each step became more difficult, and with the heat – for the sun was rising hot and fast – I had slowed to little more than a hobble.

'Let's sit,' I said.

We had been trudging up and down the valleys, with ditches and hedgerows flanking us and cattle and sheep in the fields beyond. Now, at the crest of another hill, there was an opening where a shallow stream bubbled beside a tree. I fell into the shade, grabbing at the buttons around my neck and pulling the material off my skin. I had worn the wrong dress too, and the crinoline ballooned around my legs as I sat awkwardly upon the grass.

Luella, though, seemed perfectly suited to the occasion. She crouched beside me in her white dress with the flowers on it, and her skin was just as pale as it had been in the early morning. I imagined that her feet would be fine as well in such ugly boots.

I tore off my hat, threw it away from me, and let my head rest against the tree. The breeze, which was stronger up here on the top of the hill, teased at my hair and ran its cool fingers across my scalp. I closed my eyes and drank in the air.

I had no watch upon me, so I could not be certain what Miss Grey would be doing now, but I was sure she would be awake and screaming for me. How might Cook handle the situation? She would call me names, I supposed, and tell Miss Grey that I never was any good and that Miss Grey was better off without me. Cook did not know she would have no job come Monday morning.

Ruffling, tinkling ... Luella was sifting through her cotton bag. There were few clothes inside it from what I could see – only some white material that might have been a dress or a petticoat or a handkerchief – a purse, and a flask. She had in her hand a paper bag with a chunk of bread in it.

'Want some?' She offered it to me, and I took it miserably. It must have been yesterday's lot, for it was stale.

'Water?' I said.

She ran her fingers in the stream as an answer, cupped her palm, then drank from her hand. Filthy creature. She laughed at the shock on my face.

'It's all we have,' she said, taking the bread off me and eating it all herself.

'Then I shall wait until we reach the town.' But my tongue was stuck to the roof of my mouth, and my lips were so dry that I feared they would crack. I dipped a finger into the water – at least it was cool – then ran that finger over my gums, trying not to think about the cows which drank from this same stream, nor their shit and piss which filtered into it.

'What's in that flask of yours?' I asked, for she had left her bag open, and the metal caught in the dappled sunlight. It was pewter, rather dull compared to my silver one, which now lay waiting as a snake waits for a mouse to walk between its teeth. 'You have water in there, yet you make me drink from a stream?'

The heat and exhaustion was souring my temper. It was all I could do to stop myself from calling her a selfish bitch, for it was she who had dragged me on this journey when otherwise I could have been in the carriage of a train without the pain in my feet or the ache in my hips, and she would not even share her water with me.

'It ain't water.' She scrunched the empty paper into her bag, then fastened it so I could see nothing else.

I would have pressed her on the subject, but my energy was dropping. The grass beneath me now felt soft, the moss as welcoming as a mattress. My feet and legs stuck out of the shade and were warmed by the sun. My head rested on the bark as if it were a pillow, and my eyelids struggled to stay open to look at the view of the patchwork of fields that rolled before us.

'Beautiful,' Luella whispered, and I had to agree with her, though I did not say as much. 'How old were you, Bonnie, when you went to Mrs Campbell's?'

'Twenty-two.' I recalled Frank and I walking into Bridgefield, laughing at how pretty the place was with its stone bridge over the wide river, its high street made up of Georgian buildings, and the woodlands that surrounded the place. I remembered skipping along the dirt track to the big red-brick house at the edge of the town. Its chimneys poured out smoke, the place smelt of fried bacon, and Mrs Campbell talked with me at her kitchen table as she made tea and asked if I'd like something to eat.

'How do you do it?' Luella said.

I squinted at her.

'How do you get to be their companion so easy? Everything seemed so easy for you …'

She was getting melancholy, but I was too tired to try and cheer her, so I told her the truth. 'A young, middle-class girl with a nice smile and an honest face. That's it.'

'That's what?'

'That's all I need to win them over.'

'You lie to them.'

I sighed. She was naïve for someone who had been raised as a murderer's daughter. I thought her experiences would have taught her that the world was not a fair nor a nice place to be, but who was I to tell her that now, when she had so little time left anyway?

'Yes, I lie, Luella.'

She asked no further questions. I think I dozed after that, for time seemed to jump. One minute there was sunshine, the next a cloud had passed over us. I dreamt we were riding a horse, and I woke to find Luella poking my arm and gathering up her skirt as she stepped over me towards the road. The hooves I'd heard in my dream were the hooves of a donkey pulling an old, weathered farmer on a cart.

I scrambled to my feet, pushing down my crinoline and placing my hat neatly on my head, and stepped onto the roadside, smiling.

'Excuse me, sir,' I said, stepping into the path of the donkey, 'we are heading north and wondered if you might be so kind as to let us ride with you for a while?'

The man's white brows pulled tight as he regarded us both. Luella was stroking the donkey's muzzle and whispering to it, and I thought the man must have taken her for a lunatic.

'My maid is fond of animals. She was raised a farm girl.'

The man nodded, grunted, and beckoned us to sit in the cart. He did not wait for us to be seated properly before he flicked the reins and lurched us all forward.

The cart was dirty and smelt of vegetables; it was an uncomfortable journey, but at least the weight was off my feet. I smiled at the views, as we crested hilltops and dipped into lush little valleys, until he made a right turn.

'I'm down here,' he called and stopped so we could dismount. We waved him and the donkey goodbye and trudged another mile or so until we reached an inn.

IT WAS one of those places where everyone stares at new people. The door was low, the wood dotted with iron nails and splintered so that the stench of old beer tickled you before you'd even passed over the threshold. I ventured in first, for Luella seemed to be holding back, waiting, as if she was afraid of entering a public house. She would hopefully lose her boldness again when it came time for murder.

A scruffy black dog ran at my feet, barking, and nipped my skirt. Horrible thing; it looked as if it had seen many scraps with other dogs, for half of one of its ears was missing, and there were bare, white patches of scars showing over its muzzle. I kicked it back, and a man who had propped himself up with one elbow on the bar groaned at the animal to come away. The thing didn't pay its master any heed and continued to snap at my silk skirt until Luella pushed me along and knelt before the dog. She offered her naked hand to it, and after showing her its teeth, the dog edged towards her, sniffed her fingers, licked them, then trotted away to lie down under its owner's stool.

Well, that surely got everyone's attention, didn't it? The men – for the only other female was the landlady – stared at the thin waif with a look of wary hunger in their eyes. I'd seen that look many a time, and I didn't like it being directed at Luella; in these parts, I was unsure as to whether they thought her a witch, a whore, or a simpleton.

'Sit in the corner there,' I whispered to her, giving her my case and pushing her to the place furthest away from the men, though their eyes followed her as she sat.

Raising my head, I pinned the landlady with a stare. She came forward begrudgingly, looking me up and down. Take it in, I thought, for she had likely never seen silk like my blue dress before, and I wanted her to know the sort of woman she was about to speak with.

'My maid and I will have ham and eggs, and wine,' I said. Some man to my right sniggered, but I did not turn towards him.

'Don't have wine,' the landlady said, and her accent was worse than Luella's.

'Beer, then.'

She nodded and poured us two pewter cups of it, slamming them on the counter so that the liquid sloshed over the side and splattered onto my gloves. I took no heed of her petty jealousy.

'Where might we find a coach?'

'Depends where you're wanting to get to.'

I leaned closer to the counter top and lowered my voice. 'We are heading for Bristol.'

She sniffed a dreadful, wet kind of sniff, and swallowed whatever she had taken back. 'Out of here, turn right, follow the track to the main road. Coaches pass through sometimes, though can't say if there'll be one coming today.' Then she turned and disappeared through a door, and the smell of hot fat wafted into the air.

I would have left there and then if my stomach had not been aching with hunger. The pewter cups were sticky on my gloves as I carried them to the table where Luella waited for me. She drank first, oblivious of the grubbiness, and though I tried to restrain myself, I could not stop from quenching my thirst. The beer was stale and smelt dank, but I had downed half of it before I could pull it from my lips.

'You'll be sick, carry on like that,' Luella said.

'We must be quick here, then get to the main road.' I assumed – hoped, rather – that the coachmen might be eating their own lunch somewhere now and that if we were lucky enough – and Lord, I prayed for us to be lucky, for I would not spend a night in this wretched building – we would be able to meet them for the afternoon journey.

'Where we going?'

'North.' I would not tell her the destination, for then she would have no need of me.

She nodded, placated. She was a simple girl when her anger was cold. I wondered if she might be some kind of idiot, for at times like these, nothing seemed to pass behind her eyes. She continued to gaze through the glass, which was cut so thickly that the world outside was distorted into swirls of green and blue, until the landlady dropped our plates and two grubby sets of cutlery on the table.

The ham, to my horror, was green at the edges. The egg, which had been fried, was runny on the top, the white still half transparent. Luella pierced the yolk and let it spread over her meat, then cut and sliced and shovelled it into her mouth. I decided that not a morsel of the ham would pass my lips and ate only the cooked bits of the egg.

She finished swiftly and dragged her sleeve across her lips. Then she was on her feet, waiting for me to follow. I threw a coin on the counter and followed in Luella's eager footsteps, lifting my skirts away from the dog's teeth as I jumped through the doorway.

She was ahead of me by three paces, marching over a track between some farm buildings. I had to trot to catch her, and as I did so, my foot caught in a dip, and I twisted my ankle. She caught me before I crashed onto the ground and gripped me under the armpit to hold me up. Her strength shocked me, for I was almost a head taller than her, but she appeared to have no trouble in taking my weight. Pressing into her, I limped along the track. Another dog came charging at us, and I was sure that this one, which was bigger and ownerless, would attack us, but it stopped a few feet away and only gnashed at the air as we passed.

'Hush,' Luella said, holding us both still. She cocked her head, and then I heard it too: hooves.

We hobbled as fast as we could until the track spilled onto a road, and over the tops of the hedgerows, we saw four horses dragging a coach. They were going the wrong way.

I could have cried, for the pain in my ankle was sharp, the egg and drink sloshed around my otherwise empty stomach, and the beer had made my head feel like something was sawing it open.

'When's the other one coming, going north?' Luella shouted as the coach neared us.

The driver doffed his hat to us and called back, 'Within the hour.'

The coach blew dust into our eyes as it passed. The passengers were few; I could see only one face inside the carriage, and a lad was riding at the back, letting the breeze blow through his hair.

Luella dropped me at the side of the road where the grass grew high with wildflowers. Butterflies flew out around me as I rubbed my ankle and tested how much movement it had.

It had not been a bad fall, nothing felt broken, though there was a twinge when I pointed my toes at the sky.

'How is it?' Luella lay beside me and closed her eyes against the sun.

'Fine.'

A honeybee buzzed over her, and for a moment I thought it might land on her, mistaking her for a flower, but it continued on its way. Behind her, the space above the road shimmered and waved; the sun was high in the sky.

I lay beside her. The road was quiet; just the occasional cart loaded with hay passed by, and in the distance we could hear the sounds of labourers working in the fields.

'It were raining,' Luella said. Her voice was soft and feathery. She was on the edge of sleep. 'When Pa died.'

'Was it?'

'You don't remember?'

I grunted.

'I saw you.'

I did not recall her being there. I had been watching as Samuel was walked towards the noose, my bonnet tied tight to keep the rain from my eyes. It truly had been a terrible day, an unusual cold spell for August, and the chill in the air had been like fingers down my spine.

'I were ill for weeks after that, couldn't get the wet off my lungs, like I'd breathed in all that rain.'

I wished for a drop of rain now to cool the sizzling of my face. Instead, I sat up straight and crawled into the patch of shade thrown by the hedgerow. I muttered to myself as a bramble pinched my shoulder and tugged a hole in my gown, and the crinoline dug into my thighs. Crinolines were not designed for lying in ditches.

'I'll cut your tongue out.'

I stopped and glared at Luella, uncertain of what she had just said. 'I beg your pardon?'

'What my grandmother always said if ever my ma cursed. You was cursing.'

'Was I?' We were both silent for a moment. 'Did your mother curse often?'

'Sometimes.' She seemed to wait, with something on the tip of her tongue, and a frown formed for an instant between her brows before they smoothed. 'Did you like him? My pa?'

'I thought he was a good man from the little I saw of him.'

'How often did you see him?'

When would this damned coach come? I squinted into the distance and strained to hear beyond the shouts of farmhands, but there was nothing approaching.

'When he came to the house to do the books.'

'I forget how often he went now?' She said it as a question, though I chose not to answer. 'He were gone a lot, in the end, before …'

'Yes, well.' I would not remind her of how her father had lost his job.

'And Mrs Campbell. What did you think of her?'

I blew the air out through my nose. So many questions, and I had not the energy nor the patience for them. 'She was nice.'

'She were.' Luella raised herself onto her elbows and looked at me. The sun had pinked her cheeks, darkened the freckles across the bridge of her nose. 'She were kind. She used to feed me sweets and let me see her animals. Do you remember all the animals she had?'

Too many, and Luella had been like another of Campbell's strange little pets, running and playing amidst the ramshackle flock. There'd been stray cats in the barns, donkeys which served no use, limping horses which could not pull a carriage, geese which would attack, dozens of ducks on the pond which no one could shoot for dinner, and a dog with three legs which was always by the old woman's side.

'Patch,' Luella said, smiling. 'I miss Patch. He were my favourite.'

The dog hadn't liked me, and the feeling had been mutual. It was a gnarly old thing, always licking or scratching some part of itself, and I would forever be picking its greasy hairs off the furniture.

'He died, you know, a week after she did.'

I had gone by the time Mrs Campbell died. I hadn't heard about it until years later when I'd been near the area – passing through – and I'd asked after her from someone whom I had not recognised. Her heart had worn out, apparently.

'I never saw her after Pa were arrested,' Luella said. 'She had to have a nurse look after her. The shock had done her in, see. And that nurse, well, she were a mean old goat and wouldn't let me near Mrs Campbell, not even past the gates. I suppose she thought I might have wanted to finish what my father had started.'

She laughed, the same laugh she'd made in the grocer's, the crazed kind that started and ended abruptly. She set her eyes on me, and the simpleton glaze of them that had been there at the inn was gone; she was a ferret again. 'You said Mrs Campbell were nice. She were more than nice. Did you steal off her as well?'

Who was she? A bloody judge? Looking at me down her nose like she was something more than she was. 'Yes, Luella. I stole off your dear, sweet Mrs Campbell. Shake your head at me all you like but you know me for a thief, so I doubt the news that I've always been one comes as a surprise to you.'

She smiled and nodded. 'Nothing about you will ever surprise me, Bonnie Hearn.'

I was ready to stand, to face her and call her out, for

though I'd been a lady for many years, I hadn't been born one; I knew how to take a girl down. Even with a sore ankle, I could have had her on the floor with a handful of her hair in my fist before she'd have known what was happening, but just then, the wind blew the sound of horses towards us. We turned to the road and waited with bated breath for the coach to breach the horizon.

We sat in silence inside the coach. Luella was squeezed beside a woman who tried to converse with us, but she gave up after a while. I had one side of the carriage to myself and room to spread my skirts, and I rested my cheek against the door and let the breeze from the open window cool my hot head.

I must remain in control; I must not scare her away. I said this to myself over and over, for what good would it be to lose Luella now and fear her forever?

At the next stage, Luella and I waited inside the coach as they changed the horses. The woman dismounted, muttering something about a drink and a change of company, but we were not on our own for long. A man boarded. He jumped up the steps, and we appeared to give him a shock, for he yelped when he saw us. He laughed at his outburst, doffed his cap, and then wiggled in beside Luella.

'Paul Meadows.' He removed his cap and shook out his hair which was the colour of burnt copper and just as wiry. 'Come far?'

My glare did not seem to perturb him. He continued to grin and ogle us. He had not the manners to take us in discreetly.

'Stowmouth.' Luella shifted further into her corner, but the inches she put between herself and the stranger were soon filled as he spread his legs wider.

He sucked in a breath. 'Stowmouth. Nice there. Your name?'

'Lucy,' I said before Luella could speak. 'My maid.'

Mr Meadows turned down his lips, raised his eyebrows, then guffawed and fell back against the seat, making the whole coach wobble. I poked my head through the window to see how long it would be before we were moving again and if we should dismount and take a drink at the inn just to be out of this idiot's company. However, the horses were now ready, and the driver was mounting the steps to his seat. Someone thumped the roof of the carriage, and the horses walked forward.

'Where you heading?' Mr Meadows had slid down the seat so that he could rest his head against the back of it. His feet were amidst my skirts, his knees were lolling wide, and his eyes were half closed as he gazed down at me over his nose.

'North.'

'North.' He said it mockingly, then snorted, thinking his imitation of me funny.

The fifteen miles to the next stage did not seem appealing, but I had little to worry about in the end, for Mr Meadows was sleeping before we had journeyed a mile. Though he was a horrid sight, with drool sliding from his open mouth, at least he was quiet. Luella prodded his leg off her, and he did not even stir. And though we had been sour with each other for so long, Mr Meadows at least gave us both something to laugh about.

We passed the journey taking it in turns to poke him, to tickle his nose with a piece of ribbon, to pull strands of his hair until he flinched. His grunts made us giggle, and one time, as he turned away from Luella's finger which had jabbed him in the ribs, he passed wind. The shock on both of our faces made us crease with laughter until tears were streaming down my cheeks, and both of us were shushing each other to little effect for fear that we would wake him.

It was approaching dinner time when the coach passed under the entrance arch of an inn, and the slowed pace and the sound of hooves echoing over cobblestones in the courtyard woke Mr Meadows with a start. He frowned at his surroundings, winced at some pain in his neck – he had been lying crookedly – and wiped off the spit that had slid down his chin.

And then he saw us. He scurried upright, drew his knees together, fixed his cap on his head, and blushed.

'My apologies, ladies.' He looked out of the window in horror, then patted his waistcoat pockets and, to my amazement, pulled out a watch on a chain. I had thought him nothing more than a labourer, but the watch was shiny enough, and now, with his face arranged in a sombre fashion, he did not seem as crude as he had before. He turned to us timidly.

'Do you happen to know where we are?'

CHAPTER 4

The White Hart Inn was a building pieced together with mismatched stones. Inside, it had an airless, damp feel to it, but the folk were cheerier than at the last inn, and the landlady smiled and nodded when I asked if she had a room for the night.

Mr Meadows followed us inside, his head bowed low like a scolded child. 'Please, let me buy you both dinner as an apology for …' He shook his head. I imagined he could not remember what a fool he had made of himself. Lucky him.

I accepted his offer, and Luella and I sat near the door so we could appreciate the breeze as people wandered in and out. Mr Meadows brought over wine for the three of us, and though it was bitter and watery, I was glad of the familiar taste. Luella was not so impressed, wrinkled her nose at the first sip, and did not drink again from her glass.

'May I?' Mr Meadows gestured at the seat, and I nodded. He scratched his cheek and cleared his throat. 'Sorry, I should have introduced myself.'

'You already did.'

He blushed again. 'Well, then. I am sorry, but I cannot seem to recall –'

'Miss Dayton, and my maid, Lucy.' Luella glanced at me but said nothing. I winked at her.

'Ah, yes, I remember.' He sipped some wine. 'And you are from …'

'Stowmouth.'

'Yes. Yes, of course.' He pulled off his cap and ran his hand over his hair, smoothing it this time. 'Going north.'

'That's right.'

He sighed as if he'd just passed an examination and gulped his drink. 'I beg you excuse my behaviour. I have been … well, I have been away from home for a few nights at a friend's wedding in Cornwall and …' He held up his glass of wine and laughed unsteadily.

'You are returning home?' I said. All this time, Luella said nothing. He nodded.

'And where is home?'

'Bath. I am a tailor.' He gestured at his suit, as if to prove his point, though I did not think it was something he should be all too proud about. He glanced down and saw the state of himself. He rubbed the muck off his jacket and gasped at the tear in the arm; I wondered how he would curse himself later when he noticed his trousers.

'I must apologise,' he said. 'I shall know for next time.'

HE DID NOT KNOW for next time. As the hours passed, we ate our dinners and drank wine together – beer for Luella – and ended up outside The White Hart, lounging on the grass near a footbridge as the stars twinkled in the sky. Mr Meadows held on to the bottle and swigged from it every few seconds as Luella took the branches of a weeping willow, which trailed over the little stream, and plaited them.

'I shall make you a dress of emerald green,' Mr Meadows said, his words slurring, pointing the bottle into my face. 'You shall look divine in green.' He reached for a strand of my hair but missed and fell forward onto the grass. 'Arsenic green, I think, would make you shine.'

Luella paused for a moment; both of us stilled and held our breath, then he snorted at himself.

'North. Where is north? Are you off to Scotland?'

'Perhaps.'

'Perhaps, perhaps ... what a mysterious woman you are, Miss Dayton.' He rolled towards me. His eyes were glassy, his cheeks ruddy; he drank again. 'Miss.' He hissed the word, and spit flew from his lips. 'Miss. No husband, Miss Dayton?'

I shook my head.

'A single woman, travelling all alone.' He tutted in mock disapproval.

'I am not alone. I have my maid.'

For a moment, it was as if he had forgotten all about Luella, so quiet at the edge of the group. He turned to her in surprise, then nodded and crawled towards her. Luella moved away, but he was already too close to her, and when he spoke, she turned her face from the stench of his breath.

'Lucy. Little Lucy. What a pretty little thing you are, Lucy. How old are you, Lucy?'

Luella did not answer, but glared at him.

'Come, little Lucy, smile for me. I bet you are pretty when you smile.' He touched her cheek, and she struck his hand away.

'Mr Meadows,' I said, drawing his attention away from Luella, and again he looked startled that somebody else was there with him.

'Miss Dayton! Your maid is quite a misery, isn't she? Is she ever any fun?'

I thought she would be fun when she was strangling him,

for there was such a look of fierceness in her then that I had no doubt she would have killed him if he had touched her again. And that made me think of Frank and why I had ever doubted she would have had the nerve to murder him when the time came. The thought sobered me, and I got to my feet.

'I am tired, Mr Meadows. Lucy and I are going to bed.'

He clutched at my skirt and gripped my twisted ankle. 'Do not leave me, Miss Dayton, I beg you.'

His hold was tight for a man so lost in alcohol. I kicked my feet, trying to dislodge him, but he would not loosen himself. The more I struggled, the more I hurt myself. 'Let go of me, Mr Meadows. Let go this instant.'

'Miss Dayton, you are a beautiful woman. Let me make you a green dress, hmm? Come here.' His hands slid up my calves and grasped at my stockings. I kicked him again, panicking. His hands were hot and sticky. His body was lying on the hem of my skirts so that I could not pull myself free of him. His fingers crawled higher, tickling my thigh, and his face was buried in my gown.

It was then that I screamed. I did not know I was making such a noise until Luella was beating him off me and I came back to myself. It was like everything was a dream, a nightmare, one of those nightmares where the harder you try to run, the slower you become. I stared down at Paul Meadows, who was cowering by my feet as Luella slapped and punched him into a tight ball.

Then there were other sounds: men's voices, doors opening, dogs barking. A woman ran to us and wrapped her arms around Luella to stop the violence. Mr Meadows was sobbing. My hands were shaking.

'What's going on?' It was the landlady, the kind woman who had smiled at me before about a room, who held Luella. Luella was taking deep breaths, though she looked wild. Her hair had fallen around her face, and her skin was flushed.

'This man was attacking me.' My voice came out as nothing more than a whisper. 'My maid was protecting me.'

The landlady dropped Luella and came to me, checking me over with her eyes and her hands. 'You're so cold, miss. Come and let's get you inside.'

She led me, limping, through the crowd of men who had come out to see the commotion and told them what I had told her. They let Luella through, nodding at her respectfully and fearfully, then made for Mr Meadows.

I don't know what happened to Paul Meadows once we were inside the inn. Perhaps they beat him too; perhaps they chased him off. Either way, he did not return to the inn, and I never saw him again, but we did not know that at the time.

The landlady led me upstairs to the best room they had (so she said), sat me on the bed, lit the fire in the grate, and told Luella to bring up a bottle of wine from downstairs which I could have for free.

'Did you know him?'

I shook my head. 'We met on the coach. He wanted to apologise for his drunken behaviour by buying us dinner.'

The landlady laughed. 'Nothing worse than a drunk, and I should know. I'll give him a hiding ever I see him here again. Shall I find your nightgown for you?'

'No!'

She was opening my case, and I slammed it shut on her. She jumped away, cautious now of me. 'Sorry, I am still a little on edge. My maid will help me when she returns.'

'Of course.' She brushed off her skirts, then set the key on the table beside the bed.

It was all I could do to stop myself from throwing her out and locking the door behind her.

I WAITED beside the open door, key in hand, for Luella to

return. She was slow coming up the stairs, and I almost caught her sleeve as I pushed the door shut once she had stepped into the room. Locked in, I felt I could breathe again and went to the bed to sit.

Luella put the bottle of wine on the table next to the candle and then, after hesitating, perched beside me. Below us came the muffled noise of men and women talking and drinking, and through the thin glass of the window, the sound of night in the countryside: the bubble of the stream, rustles in the hedgerows, a horse braying in the stable, a fox barking. And above it all, the throbbing of my pulse.

'Are you –'

'I'm fine,' I said. After a moment, Luella reached for the bottle, bit off the stopper, and drank. I felt her shiver before she held it out to me.

I raised the bottle to my lips and tipped it up, but my hand trembled so much that I was scared I would spill the wine. I took only one small sip, but it was enough, and the heat of the alcohol laced through me and warmed my blood.

'Thank you' – I returned the bottle to her – 'for your help.'

'Did he … Did he get to you? Properly?'

I shook my head and kept my gaze trained on the sputtering little fire. 'Quite the fighter, aren't you?'

She sniffed and swigged the wine again.

'I think we should sleep. Be ready to get off early.'

Sighing, she made her way round to me and started to take the pins out of my hair. For a moment, I was stiff; I imagined one of those pins stabbing into my neck, but she placed each one of them gently on the windowsill until my hair fell about my shoulders. Taking my hand, she helped me stand, unfastened the ties of my gown, and eased it away from me. She knelt at my feet and let me lean on her shoulder as I stepped out of my crinoline and petticoats, and then, her fingers like feathers, she rolled down my stockings, taking care over my aching ankle.

She did all this in silence whilst I remained as pliable as a doll, watching her work. Her face passed through different states, like the passing of the seasons, but I could not understand what the expressions meant, only how, at times, she reminded me so much of her father that I felt as if I had known her for years, and at other times she was the stranger whom I had only met several days ago.

Finally, she plucked out the laces of my corset, wiggled it free, then placed it neatly on the chair in the corner of the room beside the rest of my stacked clothes. From there, she faced me, and her gaze descended over my body like she was examining me for clues. I had to turn away from her, for I could feel my skin flushing.

I heard her come closer and open my case. She made no sound of surprise as the stolen trinkets tinkled amidst my gowns. She found my creased cotton nightdress without comment, then looped it over my head and pulled my arms through.

'It was my mother's husband,' I said, taking up the corner of the bed covers and slipping in between the sheets. 'He would lose something on the floor, under the table, say, and as he looked for it, he would find the time to look under my skirts as well.'

I swallowed. The explanation had been an attempt to thank her, so she would understand why I had reacted so absurdly, but it felt like I had vomited up my past, and now it lay between us, ugly and stinking, as something to be avoided. I shied away from it, pressed my cheek against the pillow, and squeezed my eyes shut.

'Did your mother not stop him?' At the foot of the bed, Luella kicked off her boots. I peeked at her and saw her delicate fingers undoing the buttons at her sleeves and watched her as she removed her gown. She held it to her chest in an embrace, then laid it out on the floor so that it seemed as if there was a third woman in the room with us.

'Mother didn't see what she didn't want to.'

A pallet bed was set up beside mine, and Luella stepped into it.

'You can sleep in here with me,' I said.

'A maid should not be in the same bed as her mistress.' There was a hint of sarcasm in her voice, then the faintest of laughs, and she slipped in beside me.

We kept good space between us. Both of us were too still, as if we didn't trust each other or ourselves. Below us, the inn door kept opening and closing as more and more men seeped out into the night and returned to their wives.

I watched the whitewashed walls flicker with the fire. The room was sparsely furnished; there was nothing good to steal, and that was the purpose of it. I liked the bareness of it – like the walls of a church, it soothed me.

'How did you meet Frank?'

His name whispered in the golden glow caused a pain to simmer under my ribs. What I would have given for it to have been him lying beside me.

'When Mother married, the last time. He was working for my stepfather as an apprentice blacksmith. My stepfather always said how he was doing Frank a favour, for his father had been a drunk and his mother a whore who'd died before he knew her. He liked to kick Frank when he made a mistake and called him Dog.'

'Why did your mother marry him? He sounds a beast.'

I laughed. Was it really hard to guess?

'Money. He'd done well for himself, though half of it was through crooked business, not that my mother minded. And he was old enough to die within a few years.'

'So he's dead now?'

'Don't know.' I hoped he was. I hoped he was rotting in the earth, that the worms had eaten through his eyeballs and had shat him out, returned him to his proper state. 'Frank and I … We saved each other, you see. We got each other out of there.'

I remembered Frank and I running out of the village, bags heavy with whatever we had managed to steal, clattering and jamming against our backs. I remembered our hands gripped together. I remembered the calluses on Frank's palms, the likes of which I'd never seen or felt before, and the burns which patterned his skin like tattoos, and how I kissed them that night as we lay at the edge of a forest, panting, sweating, laughing, crying. I remembered how the moonlight lay across his face, making his eyes as black as buttons and his skin like polished silver as we planned our future.

'You loved him,' Luella said, and her voice was flat.

Something hot bled towards my temple: a tear. I wiped it off my skin, then tucked my hand under the covers again.

'So much that it hurt.'

'I suppose love always hurts,' Luella whispered, and there was a catch in her throat. I thought perhaps she had been in love with a boy, and her heart had been broken. Or perhaps she was thinking of her father.

I WOKE AT DAWN. We had not drawn the curtains, and the sunlight stretched on to the bed, warming my legs and nudging me awake. We had less than a day's journey to Frank; if we moved now, we would be there by dinner time at the latest.

Frank would be sleeping now, I imagined. Were his dreams filled with blood and poison like mine had been? Did his stomach churn? For mine surely did when I thought of how Luella's last night alive had been spent tucked beside her killer.

Luella's lips were parted as she breathed deeply in sleep. Her head rested on the pillow with her hair spread out all around her in frizzy ringlets. Her chain was still about her neck, still hidden behind her chemise. She held her hands together before her face as if in prayer, her knuckles were grazed, and one fingernail was broken so low that the flesh had torn and bled a little. That nail was probably stuck in Paul Meadows' jacket.

I should have roused her, for she would be eager to get going, to get to Frank and kill him, but I let her sleep. There had been a softening in me towards her. If I left her sleeping, walked out of the inn and slipped away to some new place where she could never find me and Frank, then we would all be safe.

I crept out of the bed. A floorboard squeaked as I hobbled to the chair in the corner of the room. I would do without my corset and petticoats and reached only for my dress. I picked up my shoes and my bag, and with one last look at Luella, whose face now glimmered in the sunshine, I tiptoed to the door.

The key caught and clunked. Luella stirred, though her eyes remained closed. The door hinges needed oiling, but I was out on to the landing and tripping down the stairs, and still there was silence all about me.

The bar was littered with cups and glasses. Buckets full of beer and spit and tobacco oozed their stench into the room which seemed larger than it had done last night. I found a few shillings in my purse and placed them on the counter, for Luella would not have the means to pay for our stay, and I did not want the landlady fighting with her. Then I sat on a stool to put my shoes on, and in a moment, I was out of the inn.

Had it really only been yesterday that I had begun this journey with Luella? Had it only been twenty-four hours since I had left the womb-like state of Miss Grey's house? Time had seemed to stretch; a day had become a week, a lifetime. There was something like a bond which I felt with Luella now. It was because of the incident with Paul Meadows, I had no doubt – after all, she had saved me – and there I was, leading her into a trap! So yes, I was sad to creep away like that without a goodbye, but it really was the best thing to do for her, for us all.

Lifting my heels as best I could, I made my way towards the road. Over my shoulder, I checked the window of our room, but the sun reflected in the glass so that I could not see beyond it. I hoped Luella would still be sleeping. I hoped her grazes would heal, and as they healed, I hoped she would forget about me and Frank. I hoped she would never see me again.

I would walk all the way to Frank if I must; I could not risk meeting Luella in a stagecoach, for no doubt she would come looking for me. It would take me days to reach him if I could not beg a lift, but I thought someone would take pity on a crippled woman who could pay them in silver for their kindness.

And it was when I was imagining what I would say to a passer-by – some sad story of how I had fallen and no good Christian had cared to help me – that I was startled by a voice.

'Bonnie?'

Behind me, her dress dragged carelessly over her head so that the hem of it was turned up around her knees and her hair was stuck out on one side, Luella trotted towards me. She stopped a few feet away, and I had to look at the ground so I did not see the disappointment in her face.

'You was leaving me.'

There was a stone near the tip of my shoe, and I kicked it into the ditch. 'It is better this way.'

'You promised me you would take me to him.'

'It is a bad business, Luella. Bad things will happen.'

'What about the boat? What about being free?'

'You are free now, Luella. You are free to go from here as an innocent, without the stain of murder on your conscience. Can't you see?' I stepped towards her, reached for her, but she flinched out of my grasp. 'I am trying to help you.'

She waited, and I was sure that she was doubting herself. Her frown was deep, her eyes wide. I took the chance to persuade her more and dropped my bag on the ground, retrieved my purse, and showed her the five-pound note.

'Have this. Take it and go to Bristol, to the docks there. Board a ship to America like we said we would. Start again, Luella, free of sin. Start a new life and forget about me, forget about Frank.'

'My father,' she whispered, and her hand fluttered to her chest. The chain had worked free of her bodice so that I could see the locket which dangled from it. Samuel's likeness must have been in there, and the thought made my skin crawl.

'Forget about your father! His death, I mean. Take the memories with you, the happy ones. You cannot bring him back, you cannot change what has already happened, but you can change what is about to happen.'

She was not looking at me, but staring blindly into the distance as she clutched the locket. I held my breath, too scared to breathe in case I roused her from the dream of freedom in America. And I was just about relaxing, thinking I had done it, thinking that I had changed her mind, changed our fates and saved us all, when her gaze returned to me.

There are always choices in our lives. I have often looked at life as I would look at a map and seen the roads cross and diverge and separate. Each direction takes us somewhere different, and our decisions lead us unknowingly to our destinations.

Luella could have taken us all on a different path; instead she continued on a doomed journey, forcing us all along with her.

She thrust the money back at me. 'Take me to Frank.'

I opened my mouth to try to reason again, but she spoke above me.

'Take me to Frank, Bonnie, as you promised you would. You owe me, remember?'

She was referring to last night, and now I knew why she had defended me so valiantly; it was a weapon to use against me. I felt the treachery deep inside, a knife of sickness through my stomach.

She trudged towards the inn. 'Come on, I'll help you dress properly, and then we leave.'

AFTER BREAKFAST of a boiled egg and toast, we mounted the stagecoach. Neither of us was speaking to the other. I turned my face to look at the view while Luella closed her eyes and feigned sleep.

We were alone in the carriage. No one bothered much with stagecoaches because of the railways, and though I had been against the idea initially, I was grateful to be away from the bustle of train crowds with just Luella and my thoughts and guilt, for it meant I did not have to pretend quite so much. And, of course, the journey was slower and gave Frank more time to prepare.

The land grew flatter, and we could see for miles over the chequerboard pattern of fields, the majority of which were a golden colour, like patches of sand, for the hay was drying in the sunshine. The heat built as the morning passed until I had to use my hat to fan my face. Luella woke as the breeze caught her flushed skin, and she rearranged herself, pulling at the material under her armpit so that I could see the dark patch of sweat there.

'Where are we?' she asked, her voice thick as she licked her lips.

I shrugged. I was loath to talk to her.

She pushed herself towards the window, cast her face out into the air, and breathed in deeply. 'We are close.'

'Close to where?'

'Bridgefield.'

I had hoped we would pass the turning for her hometown before she woke. Begrudgingly, I nodded.

'Want to call in?' She did not respond to the acidity in my voice. 'Tell them all what you're planning?'

She rolled her eyes to the sky. 'Don't be childish.'

'It is not me who is the child here.' She was ignoring me now and staring out of the other window. 'How old are you, anyway?'

'Eighteen.'

'Christ. So you were how old when …'

'Ten. Just. It'd been my birthday the week he got arrested.'

Sickness waved through me. A child. To see her father die, to see the hangman, to be left …

'What happened to you after? Where did you go?'

'To live with my grandmother. She's at the edge of the town by the woods, a squat little cottage where the rain runs inside the walls in winter.' She threw her words like pins, seeing which would make me squeal.

'In summer, though, it must be pretty.'

'Oh yes, very pretty, you're right. Grandma has a garden around her cottage, and the most beautiful flowers grow there. Flowers of all colours: sunshine yellow, sapphire blue, and blood-red, all coming out to say hello. The red ones are my favourite.'

She had grown odd again. Her lips were peeled over her teeth, white from their dryness but streaked with lines of red where the skin was cracking. Her eyes glittered from within, and the sight of her made my stomach turn.

'Should you like some water, Bonnie? You look queer.'

'You have water?'

'No.' She laughed, cackled rather. 'But you'd like some. Maybe we should stop at the next inn we see. We could have a feast, a last supper, if you like! If I'd've known you had five pounds on you, I would've drunk rum and port last night and chucked shillings at that Meadows bloke's eyes to stop him tickling you.'

I wondered if she had not already been on the rum, for it sounded like it. 'Tickling me, you say?'

She shrugged. 'Just a word for it. Pa would say that he were having a tickle with Ma when I were a little 'un. Just a little tickle.' She ran her fingers over my knee and laughed when I hit her hand away. 'You have a tickle with Frank, back when you loved him?'

'Luella, calm down. You are embarrassing yourself.'

She slumped against her seat and pouted, and in the next instant, the lunatic glint had disappeared, and she was morose once again. 'Grandma said that's all men want, to have a good tickle. Is that right, Bonnie?'

'Why are you asking me?'

'Because I think you'll tell me honestly.'

Honestly? Wasn't it only yesterday that she was chiding me for thieving, and no thief that I've known has ever been called honest. 'Most men, yes. But some, I think not. I think some value love more than just tickling, as you call it.'

'Really?'

She was examining me again, searching for a reaction.

Beads of sweat were building at my hairline. 'Have you a handkerchief?'

Luella opened her bag and took out a patch of cotton. She held it for a moment, unsure whether to part with it, then leaning forward, her eyes pinned on me, she held it out. I thought perhaps there was something on it like a stain of blood or mucus that she was embarrassed to show me, and for a moment, I too wavered before I felt one bead trickle down my forehead. I snatched it from her without looking at it and wiped my face, and still she stared. It was then that I glanced at the plain white cotton, and then, with a sudden rush that almost made me gasp – but not quite – I saw the name, embroidered in red stitches, in the corner.

Somehow, I remained silent. The air was taut between us.

'He dropped it when he were being arrested. It were dirty from all the boots what trampled it, but we saved it.'

'We?' My voice was nothing more than a breath.

'Ma and me. Neither of us wanted to wash it. It smelt of him, see. We kept it crumpled and filthy for months, long after he'd gone.'

'It's clean now.'

'Grandma.' She spat the word.

I tore my eyes away from it and made myself smile, though I think it must have looked more like a grimace, for it surely felt painful. 'At least you have something to remember him by.'

Luella took it from my fingertips and dropped it into her bag again. 'Yes, it really is the perfect thing to remember my pa by.'

'And your locket too,' I said, trying to be light. 'You keep a part of him close to your heart always.'

She took the locket in her hand and opened it so that only she could see. 'This is all for you,' she whispered, then pinched it shut. 'How long until we reach Frank?'

CHAPTER 5

I'd had my eyes shut for the last several miles and had been thinking of winters and snow and ice on the windows, trying to cool myself, when the scent of the sea roused me. Peering out of the window, I could see that the land around us was shallow, and the road we journeyed along seemed to have sunk into the earth.

We were close.

I thumped the roof of the coach. 'Is there an inn nearby?'

The driver's voice boomed back. 'Less than a mile.'

Luella sat up straight and clutched her bag. 'This it?'

'Not quite. I need rest first.'

'You've been resting all morning.'

'You will have to wait!' I pinched the bridge of my nose; I had a headache building behind my eyes.

We dismounted outside a half-timber-framed building where a wooden sign with a picture of an oak tree upon it hung under one of the casement windows. A cat stretched in the sunshine on the grass before the door, lifted its head, and squinted at us as we passed. Luella cooed at it, and it meowed back at her.

The Royal Oak was quiet inside, and the landlord jumped to greet us, his only customers. He made us up a table by the large window which overlooked the road, and Luella was pleased that she could watch the cat from her seat. The landlord brought us a jug of water, gave us his best glasses and a bottle of wine, and offered us napkins which looked as if they hadn't been out of their locked cupboard for years. He was disappointed when I asked only for bread and salted butter – my stomach needed something plain to ease its nausea – and insisted on bringing us thick slices of ham and a salad picked from his vegetable patch only that morning.

'And have you a room for the night?'

'Oh yes! Absolutely!' He ran out, and his footsteps pounded on the stairs. Above us, there was the sound of a bed being made, a window being flung open, objects being hammered to release the dust.

'You said we wasn't far. Why are we waiting another night?'

'Because …' My headache was worsening. The glare from the sun outside stabbed into my eyes. 'Because I cannot do it today, Luella. Forgive me, but I cannot. Tomorrow, a new day, and I promise you, we will go to Frank.'

She rose and, taking a leaf of lettuce with her, strolled out of the inn. I watched her through squinted eyes as she sat on the grass beside the cat which stood to meet her and wrapped itself around her torso, headbutting her and purring so loudly that I could hear it through the glass.

I picked the soft middle out of my slice of bread and rolled it tight between my fingers.

What had I been thinking? To murder … to plot a girl's murder! How had I become so wicked?

Perhaps the more one tells oneself they are evil, the more they truly become it.

I could not look at her. I could not look at the food on my

plate. I closed my eyes and tried to think of Frank, to think of him dead, to think of him arrested, to think of him swinging on the end of a rope ... and as I saw my Frank's body blowing in the wind, the vision morphed to one from eight years ago. Samuel, the hangman pulling on his legs, and the scream somewhere beyond my vision, the like of which I'd never heard before and hadn't heard since: the wail of someone's world being destroyed.

The landlord stumbled downstairs, breathless, his cheeks red and glistening. 'All ready for you, madam. It's our best room, fresh flowers, privy just out the back.'

'Yes, yes, thank you.' I stalked over to him at such a pace that he jumped behind the bar away from me as if I might attack him. 'Have you paper? And pen and ink?'

He scratched at his ear and gazed about himself as if expecting to see the items miraculously appear beside the bottles of rum and gin. 'I might have some upstairs.'

'Go and fetch it then.' I shooed him upstairs and followed closely behind, waiting at the door to the best room as he rummaged in his own cramped quarters. There was a muffled cry, perhaps a child or a disturbed cat, then he came towards me.

'This is all I can find.'

The paper was thin and had some kind of tally of expenses on one side of it. My haste made it tear under the nib of the pen, and the ink was low in the pot and almost dried out so that my writing was spotted and unclear, but Frank would understand well enough.

'Wait!' I said as he was about to return downstairs.

I folded the note four times until it was as small as the tip of my finger, and then I went to the landlord, whose gaze was firmly planted on the floor. Taking his hand, I wrapped his fingers around the note and pressed hard.

'You will take this to Ulstone this afternoon – this

minute. You will take it to the blacksmith there and give it to no one but him, you understand?'

He nodded, and his eyes flicked up to me. 'Who will look after the inn?'

I would have cursed at him, but I bit my lip just in time. My tooth took off a sheath of skin, and I tasted the tang of blood on my tongue. He saw this and winced, and his eyes slipped sideways, then back to me, then sideways again, and I wondered if he thought me some kind of lunatic escaped from the asylum.

I breathed in, and over the clutch of pain in my forehead, I smiled at him. 'What is your name?'

The question confused him, and after a moment of thought, he said, 'David Roberts.'

I still held his hand – I had been squeezing it hard. I loosened my grip and caressed my thumb over his fingers. 'David, you have been kind to me. The salad really was delicious.'

A smile tilted his lips. I edged a little closer and lowered my voice. 'It is an unusual request, I know, but you would be doing me a wonderful favour if you could take this note, for it is rather urgent, I am afraid. I would go myself, but I have been travelling for so long already, and I am so tired and so warm.' My hand left his and came to my throat, where I unplucked the buttons about my neck. His eyes followed. 'I need to rest. I need to lie down.'

He nodded slowly.

'My maid will take care of things downstairs while you are gone.'

'It'll take a few hours,' he said, but there was no protest in his voice now.

'As long as you deliver it today. And when you get back, I should like to buy your best bottle of wine, and I should like you to drink with me.'

'Thank you, madam, very kind of you.' He licked his lips but made no attempt to move.

Patting his hand, I kissed him on the cheek; he smelt of sweat and wood smoke. 'You must hurry now, David.'

Blushing, he turned to head on his journey.

'David.' I stopped him as he was halfway down the stairs. 'I trust you will not open the note. It is private, you see, and the man whom you are to deliver it to will know if anyone but me has seen it. He likes things kept private, that man, and has been known for his temper. You will not anger him, will you, by opening the note? I should be so upset if he was to hurt you.'

'No, madam, no. Of course I shan't open it.' He lifted it before him, as if to show me exactly what he was doing, and carefully placed it in the pocket inside his jacket. 'No one shall see it, madam, I give you my word.'

I let my eyes mist. 'Thank you, David. And go through the back door, won't you, so as not to disturb my maid?'

He nodded.

'I knew you were a good man. As soon as I saw you, I knew it. I shall be waiting for your return.'

Another wash of blood to his cheeks, then David was running down the stairs. From the casement window a few moments later I saw him making for the road. He had taken the back door and was hidden by the hedgerows which only I, from this vantage point, could see over. Poor man, his lungs would be blown out if he continued like that the whole way to Ulstone!

I slipped my chain out from under my dress. The gold wedding band was hot where it had been against my skin. I pressed it to my lips in a kiss and whispered to the wind to make David quick and sure on his journey, as below me Luella talked nonsense to the cat.

I WOKE to find Luella glaring down at me. Pushing myself upright and rubbing the sleep from my eyes, I saw how the sun had slipped lower in the sky, its honey-coloured rays making long shadows of the hedgerows, illuminating the palest line of blue on the horizon. Had David reached Ulstone yet?

'You was talking,' Luella said. She was sitting on the bed, and it took me a while to realise what the strange noise in the room was: the cat. It had curled into a ball on the pillow beside me. Luella was stroking it, making its moulting fur filter through the air and land on my face. I scowled at the creature which gazed back at me without a care.

'What was I saying?' My mouth had that dreadful stale taste, and as I ran my tongue over my gums, I dislodged a soggy crust of bread from between my teeth.

'He's gone,' Luella said, ignoring my question. 'The landlord. I can't find him nowhere.'

'What do you want him for?'

She shrugged and curled the cat's tail around her finger.

'Perhaps he has some business elsewhere. He will be back for dinner tonight.'

'How do you know?'

'We haven't paid him yet.'

There was a glass of water on the table. Luella must have brought it up for me. I sipped it gratefully, smiling at her, but she was looking at my chest, for the chain was loose, and the ring shimmered brightly against the blue of my gown.

'What's it like to be in love, Bonnie?'

She was melancholy. Too long in the sun, I guessed. 'We talked about that yesterday.'

'Love hurts, you said, and I can believe that. But there must be more. There must be joy. Why would anyone do it if there were no joy in it?'

She was a strange girl. I had never known anyone so intent on murder and revenge, and with such a naïve heart.

'There is joy,' I said, for I could not stop myself; the sadness in her face, the confusion that always seemed to plague her, made me want to make her understand. 'There is nothing better in the whole world than to love and be loved in return.'

'Love is when you'll do anything for someone, ain't it? Like die for them.'

'Yes,' I whispered.

Luella's fingers trailed from the cat's head to the tip of its tail. 'And what makes you love somebody?'

I searched for an answer but could not find one. 'There is no logic to it.'

'So we can love the wrong people? Like you loved Frank, and he were the wrong person?'

A part of me wished to strike her whenever she said his name. Another part of me wanted to tell her the truth, that I loved him still, and to beg her for forgiveness, for how were we to know back then what would have become of her? How were we to know she would have grown into such a damaged woman? Fathers die all the time. Fathers are unknown, unwanted, absent, and daughters do not turn out like Luella.

'I never knew my father,' I said. Her hand faltered, and the cat raised its head to remind her to continue fussing it. 'Not even his name. Hearn was the name of the man my mother married after I was born. For three years, I was just Bonnie. All I know is that he came on a ship from some hot country, for my mother was as pale as you, and was gone on it again before the sun had risen.'

'Do you think of him?'

'Only when I look at the sea. I've always liked it, you know, and I've wondered if that is a bit of him in me. Mother got sick just crossing a bridge.'

'You'd like to find him?'

I shook my head. 'What would be the point? I might not like what I find. Sometimes it's better just to dream and leave it at that.'

She nodded, and frowned at the embroidery on the bedspread. Something passed behind her eyes: clouds of thoughts. The cat's purrs grew softer as it slipped into sleep, and Luella was steeped in a beam of gold from the setting sun as she clutched her locket.

'Bonnie.' Her voice was low and almost inaudible, but her gaze, when it finally left the bedspread, pierced into me. 'Bonnie, I think you're right. What you said before, about being free. I should like to be free, Bonnie.'

I reached for her, leant close to her so that our faces were inches apart. My voice came out feverishly. 'Be free, Luella. Go now; take the money I have and go to the docks. Never think of us again. Have a new life. Find a man to love. There will be a ship sailing in the morning, no doubt –'

'But I must know.'

I stopped my rushing words. *Do not scare her away!* I inhaled slowly. 'What must you know?'

Her hands slipped off the locket and came to mine. They were hot and damp as if there was a fire burning within her which she was struggling to contain. 'Please, Bonnie. Tell me the truth and I'll go. I promise I'll go before the clock strikes the next hour. I don't want to harm no one' – her eyes swelled with tears – 'but I must hear the truth so that I can rest. So that we can both rest and know the truth has been spoken, is known, and is regretted.'

My ribs pounded, for my heart was beating so fast.

A tear dropped over the rim of her eye and ran down her cheek. 'What happened the night Mrs Campbell's nephew died?'

Could I say it? I hadn't even been able to think of it these last few years; I had managed to hide it away in the furthest corner of my mind so that it came out only during my nightmares.

The truth.

It was a chain around my heart squeezing the life from me. But to let one person hear it, the only person to whom it mattered, would it free me? How long had I locked it away where it could not escape? It had stayed a secret for so long I was not sure that I could ever find the key to free it.

'Nicholas Campbell.' The name alone was like a boulder off my tongue. 'He was a nasty man. He didn't do a thing for his aunt, but it was his name on her house, her accounts, her allowances.'

'He inherited the Campbell carpet factory from his uncle, I know.'

'And you know it was him who sacked your father?'

She nodded. 'Said he'd been fiddling the books. Said he'd been stealing, but we never saw no money.'

The sun had spread to me and was burning my skin. I pressed the back of my hand to my cheek. 'Well, anyway, Nicholas got rid of your father, and one night I found him in the study – heard him – heard something scratching in there. I thought it might have been Samuel returned –'

'What for? Why would my father have returned?'

'I don't know.' I cleared my throat, swallowed. 'Anyway, I opened the door and found Nicholas. He'd been drinking, I could smell it in the room – your father never drank, did he? Yes, so I found him in there, looking things over, and I was about to shut the door on him and leave him to his business, but he'd seen me by then. He was in such a foul temper and green with drink. He' – I breathed in – 'he came for me, and ... and he ... tickled me, as you say. He tried to, at least.'

I dared not look Luella in the eye. Instead, I gazed at her locket and wondered if corpses really could turn in their graves. 'I fought him. I was vicious; I did all I could. Frank must have heard it. I didn't know he was there until Nicholas fell away from me. Frank used a poker from the fire. Ever such a mess everywhere.'

I bit my lip and took a chance; I looked up. Luella's blue eyes seemed to wobble because of all the water in them. Her chin, too, wriggled, but she contained herself.

'I didn't know what else to do, Luella, who else to turn to. Samuel was a kind man, I knew it, and he knew the town and the people. I thought he could help.'

'You called for him,' she whispered.

'I did, yes. I wish now that I had not. I wish now that I had never opened that study door. But I did. Samuel came and saw everything.' I chewed my lip, hard, felt the blades of my teeth slice through my own flesh and did not look up. 'I didn't know they would blame it on him. They said he had reason to do it, that there was blood on him when they went for him the next day after they found the body. That Nicholas was in the study proved it further, so they said. And, well, Nicholas had just sacked him; he had every reason to do it.'

'Except he didn't, did he?'

I couldn't answer her.

'You let my pa die.'

Her words struck my heart, for that was the truth of it. I had watched as his life had spluttered and gushed out of him; hanging was the most degrading of deaths.

Shame enveloped me. 'He was a good man, your father. I want you to know that.'

Luella was cold, steely, changed. I peeked at her and saw that her tears had dried, that her chin was still, that her fist was white as she gripped the locket. There was a creak in her neck as she nodded mechanically. 'And that is the truth? That is exactly what happened?'

'That is the truth.'

Then she screamed.

She shook with it, her mouth stretched wide, her lips cracking and bleeding, until she had no breath left in her lungs. The cat leapt off the bed and sprinted out of the room, and then Luella fell forward, smothered her face with the pillow, and sobbed.

As her body roiled and jolted, I reached for her and touched her arm. At the feel of me, she stopped and held herself stiff.

'Luella? Luella, I am sorry. I am so sorry. Now you know.'

She pulled her arm away from me and pushed herself upright. She threw her legs off the bed so that her back was to me. Her hair frizzed all around her head, and she wiped her face with her hands. She got to her feet, patted down her skirt and gently, as if it hurt her to do so, walked out of the room.

'Now I know.'

I SAT VERY STILL and listened. I heard her run down the stairs, the door of the pub open, and her skirt brush over the grass. Creeping to the window, there was no sign of her outside. The cat now slept on the bench; the wood must have held the sun's warmth. The sun itself hung low on the horizon like a giant peach, its juices oozing over the landscape, drowning everything in gold.

I returned to the bed. Perhaps that was it; perhaps she had gone just as quickly and as absurdly as she'd arrived. Perhaps I would never see her again. The money remained in my bag, but Luella never seemed interested in money anyway.

There was no use trying to understand her. I would have to wait and pray and hope that the landlord would be back soon and tell me more good news so that I could sleep soundly.

He came within the hour, puffing and panting. His linen shirt hung off him in dark folds where the sweat had dragged it down, and his jacket was looped over his arm. I was waiting for him downstairs with a pint of beer ready. He took it off me eagerly and drank it all in six gulps, then put the glass on the bar, wiped his lips, and burped.

'Manners,' he said, patting his chest.

'Did you do it? Did you give the note to the blacksmith?'

'I did.'

'And?'

He frowned.

'What did the blacksmith say? Did he read it?'

'I don't know. I didn't stick around long enough. He showed me out, and what with you saying he had a temper, I thought I best do as he wanted.'

I smiled instead of spitting at him as I wished to do. There was no point getting angry with him. Frank had the note, and that was all that mattered. I breathed deeply, sighed in relief. All would be well now if Frank did as I said. All would be well come the morning.

'Thank you, David. And home before the sun has gone down – how you must have run!'

'I did, madam, I did. For you.'

A timid look came to his eye, with a slither of coyness that did not suit a man of his years and grubbiness.

'Then you better make us dinner and find your best wine.'

He scuffled behind the bar and brought out a bottle. 'Shall your maid be dining as well?'

'She is out for the evening.'

'Just the two of us then.'

He was hopeful, I gave him that, and stupid if he thought dinner would lead anywhere else. I grabbed the wine and drank straight from the bottle, hoping the night would soon be over.

I WOKE TO BIRDSONG. My head was stuffy, my mouth dry. I could taste the wine and onions from dinner last night, and as I rolled my head to one side, I caught the smell of tobacco on my hair and remembered David's pipe, the puckering of his wet lips, the weakness of his hand as I pushed him away. I'd left him around midnight alone beside the wood fire, for he'd barred the door in case anyone had tried to disturb us. I'd left him with a kiss on his cheek and a pound note in his hand and had locked my bedroom door.

Now, all was quiet but for David's snores coming from a few rooms down the landing. I tiptoed out of bed, found a clean dress from my bag, and readied myself for the day.

The sky outside was cloudier than yesterday; the sun had not managed to break through. As I opened the window, the air was still and a little chill – a better day for travelling.

From my case, I took a silver ring holder and placed it on my pillow for David to find whenever he woke, which I imagined would not be for some hours. Then, silently, I made my way downstairs.

The door was bolted and the iron groaned as I shoved it open; at least I knew Luella had not returned.

The cat found me as I made for the road. It was bright-eyed after a night of hunting and twisted around my legs, manically headbutting my skirts until I gave it a quick pat; I was feeling perkier today. It abandoned me once I was on the road, stalked up to one of the bushes, watched a blackbird scuffle in the undergrowth, and lowered itself on its haunches.

I turned my head before I saw it pounce. I would have no death today. I would have no ugliness, no violence, only happiness. For wasn't it a lovely day? Luella was gone. The breeze was cool. My ankle no longer ached as it had, only twinged now and again when I stepped too hard. And I would be with Frank before night came, at the docks, about to set sail across the sea.

Yet, as I walked, my mind continued to drift to thoughts of Luella. Where had she disappeared to? I imagined her walking under the moonlight and some old lady peeping from her window and thinking she had seen a ghost gliding along the road. I imagined her bumping into that dreadful man, Paul Meadows, drunk in some ditch somewhere, dragging her in beside him. I imagined her being set upon by a stray dog, being bitten by a cat, being chased by a gang of boys, for there really was no safety in being alone when one was so young and beautiful.

Then I shook my head. It was Luella, after all. She would charm any animal she met and batter any man who tried to overpower her. It was I, alone with a weak ankle, who should be worried about walking in the dawn light.

Above me, a chatter of starlings fluttered against the pale sky. Houses speckled the landscape along the roadside, some big with fields of crops around them, some small and standing like soldiers in terraces. It was a quiet part of the country and sombre at that time of the day. Eerie, even. The sound of my heels on the road echoed around me, and I pulled my shawl a little tighter against my exposed neck.

I walked until the houses disappeared and the hedgerows grew denser. I could not see through the briars and foliage to what was beyond. The smell of the sea, of hay, of manure, only disorientated me further.

Of course I was on the right road, I told myself. There was no other road. But walking with nothing but green all around and white above can leave one feeling rather lost.

I hummed my mother's tune to fill the silence but kept

my ears pricked for any unusual noise. Once, a pigeon flapped over the hedgerow and made me scream. I forced myself to laugh at my nervousness, for if I did not laugh, I would have continued to scream.

With a hand on my racing heart, I pushed on and bizarrely found myself wishing that Luella was with me. Odd company she had been, but company nonetheless. Funny how in only a matter of days I had come to expect to see her beside me wearing that pretty scowl of hers and to hear her thick accent that dropped aitches and elongated vowels.

I wondered again how it would feel to call her daughter. Of course, she was too old to be my daughter. But still I pretended; I played a game in my head and saw her face again, not as that of a stranger, but as one belonging to me. I remembered her hot little hands, and I imagined what it would feel like if her flesh was my own flesh. I recalled patting her arm, the thinness of her cotton dress, the way she shook as she sobbed, and I imagined that I had scooped her into my arms and whispered that everything would be all right until she believed me.

Then the air went from my lungs. I had to lean against a tree for I had not the strength to stand by myself. My cheeks were sopping as tears came thick and fast from my eyes. The more I told myself to stop, to collect myself, to be as bonnie as my namesake, the more I wept.

I placed my outspread fingers on my stomach and imagined it rounded. To have something growing inside me, something that I could have all to myself and love forever, wouldn't it be magical? But magic didn't exist.

I thought of the lies that I had told, and how they had poisoned me from within. I could not bear a child. No matter how much I would love and cherish it, I was my mother's daughter, after all. My heart could not stretch further than myself and silver coins. My body rejected everything else, so it seemed.

In that moment I realised what a burden I must have been to my mother. A lump of flesh stuck to her, reminding her of her shame, of all the lies she had ever told and all the foolish mistakes she had ever made. No wonder she struck me so often and let her husbands do what they wanted with me; I would have treated something I despised in the same way.

How she must have rejoiced when she woke to find me gone! The stolen money would have been a small price to pay for such a big reward. I had thought, these past twelve years, that she had been looking for me to make me pay for my betrayal of her and her husband. How often had I woken in the night, my heart pounding, thinking I heard her footsteps on the other side of the door come to punish me? What a fool I had been. Why would she ever have come looking for me? My disappearance was the thing she most desired.

I sniffed and wiped my face with my sleeves; the mauve silk blotted to violet. Looking around, I saw that my imagination had run away with me. There was only the emptiness of a Somerset road in the early morning, only blue tits and blackbirds and pigeons waking for the day, only clouds mottled grey with long overdue rain. There was nothing and no one to fear, for I was all alone, as I had been forever. As I would be for the rest of my life.

I carried on walking.

CHAPTER 6

I had travelled perhaps a couple of miles, though it had taken longer than it should have done because of my gentle steps, when there came a rumbling in the distance.

Wheels. Hooves.

I had come to an area where the hedgerows had vanished, and all about me the sky loomed like a cast of steel and made the verdant fields appear murky and dull. I waited, hoping for a coach, and silently thanked God when I saw one coming my way. I thought, what with things having gone so well recently, that I might take up Christianity again, visit a church on Sunday and see how things had changed since I'd last been to a service.

I was thinking this, and what outfit I might wear and whether the soles of my feet would sizzle as I stepped on to hallowed ground, as the stagecoach driver slowed his horses to a walk and came to a stop in front of me.

Poor man. He was thin and old, and I wondered how he had seen his wages diminish over the years. Nevertheless, he smiled and hobbled off his seat to help me with my case, asking as he did so in his shaky voice where I had come from.

'Strange for a lady like yourself to be walking alone at this hour, miss,' he said, fixing my case to the roof. He offered me his hand to help me inside the carriage. 'And where is it you be heading to?'

'Ulstone.'

Suddenly I had the most peculiar sensation. It might have been the smell, the tang of carbolic soap and salt that I had never noticed before. It might have been the catch of a yellow flower – a bright colour striking my eye on such a bleak day. It might have been the driver saying I'd have some female company for my journey. It might have been anything, but all of a sudden there was a feeling like a blunt blade scraping over my skin, and I knew, before I looked inside, that Luella was in the carriage.

The driver shut the door. It caught on my crinoline and bowled me inside. I stumbled for a moment, and Luella grasped my arm to steady me, then took it away quickly once I was sorted.

I sat opposite her and said nothing until the driver flicked his reins and the horses walked on. From this height, I could see the grey sea to my left, coming nearer. My time was running out.

'You didn't take the money. I can get it from my case. We'll ask him to stop, shall we?' I raised my fist ready to bump on the roof, but Luella shook her head. 'Where have you been all night?' I scanned her clothes, searching for mud and twigs and hay, but found she was just the same as always: slightly dishevelled, but so that it suited her.

She shrugged and said nothing.

'I was worried about you.'

She sniggered, and I blushed. What was the point in trying to reason with her? I turned my face to the view. A single seagull flew parallel to us, its wings shaped like a perfect arrowhead, and it let out a sharp, high cry.

'Did you sleep with the landlord?'

I was not shocked by her bitterness and did not flinch at her acidity. 'No, I did not.'

'I saw him coming back, running like a duck and sweating. Where had he been?'

I shrugged.

'Where did you send him?'

'That really is none of your business, is it, Luella? Not anymore.'

'Love is supposed to blind you, ain't it?'

I clenched my teeth together – another conversation about love. Really, what was wrong with the girl? She was obsessed with it.

'I have no time for this Luella –'

'Why, where are you going? Are you getting off soon?'

'That is not what I meant.'

'Then you have time to listen. What else will you do?'

I folded my arms and turned away from her, making it clear that she could speak all she liked, but I would do my damnedest to ignore her.

'I didn't understand that saying when I were little. I had a nightmare one time about loving my ma and waking up and only seeing darkness, and I thought I best not love her too much. I shied away from her hugs for years, and after a while she stopped trying.'

She sniffed, and dabbed her eyes with her fingers, but I did not try to comfort her.

'How I wish I'd had them hugs now. You never asked about her, you know. All this time and you've never asked about my mother.'

An image flashed in my mind: Mrs Blyth. Luella was the spit of her. She was a beauty, even in black crepe.

I did not like the catch in Luella's voice. She was on the edge of her emotions, and I thought she might scream like she had last night if she talked too much of family. I could not be doing with the hassle this morning when I was so nearly rid of her. I closed my eyes and pursed my lips, and after a moment I heard Luella rub her sleeve against her face. When she next spoke, she was calm.

'It's why people don't see the betrayal coming, ain't it? Because they're blind with love. They can't see how they've been used.'

Though there was no breeze, a chill drenched my body. The skin on my arms was raised in gooseflesh; I shivered and opened my eyes. Luella was staring at me.

'You will take me to Frank.'

'That is not what we agreed. You said you would leave if I told you the truth.'

'Take me to him.'

'You gave me your word, Luella.' My voice was rising. I held on to the seat to stop me lunging at her. 'You want to be free. Go and be free. You promised me you would leave.'

'Changed my mind.'

'I am doing this for you!' My hand flew to my mouth, trying to catch the words before they came out, but it was too late. The driver shouted to ask if everything was all right, and I shouted back that everything was fine.

'I am doing this to save your soul, Luella.'

'You should think about your own soul. It's no good trying to save someone else's.'

I breathed in deeply, though there was an ache inside me as if she'd kicked me in the gut. 'I won't take you, Luella. Go to the police if you like. They'll never believe you. Shout it at all the people you meet for all I care; they will take you to the asylum before they go knocking on Frank's door. I refuse to take you to him. You won't find him.'

She sighed, and the bruises under her eyes showed how tired she was. 'He is in Ulstone. That is where you are headed, you said so to the coachman. That is where I shall find Frank.'

I cursed under my breath and cursed God too for He had only been playing me; He was never on my side at all.

'Fine.' I fell back against my seat, defeated. Outside, the seagull had vanished and the sky was darkening; the storm was near. 'But you will remember that I tried to save you, Luella. You will remember that.'

'STOP HERE, PLEASE.'

The coach slowed. 'Not at Ulstone yet, miss,' the driver shouted but stopped anyway and came to open the door.

'I should like the walk.' I gave him more money than the journey warranted, and his eyes misted a little as he took it and helped me with my case.

'You too?' he said. I followed his gaze to find Luella dismounting, clasping her bag near her chest.

'Want some fresh air,' she said.

He wasn't as nice to Luella, who counted out the exact fair and gave not a halfpenny more. He bid me good day and, without a glance at Luella, mounted his seat and continued onwards.

'You should have stayed on until Ulstone. It will look odd for you to walk with me.'

'And arrive at Ulstone and find you not there? Hiding from me? I ain't letting you out my sight again, Bonnie. You've got the poison.'

We walked at a distance from each other, Luella stalking several paces behind me. Even so, when we spoke, we did so in whispers, for the land had sprouted clusters of trees and we both thought – so I imagined – that there might be spies behind them.

'Why are we walking there anyway? The coach drives straight through the place.'

'Oh yes, we should have just hopped off and shouted our arrival to the whole village. Hello, we've come to kill a man – your blacksmith, as it happens!'

'Mock me, I don't care.'

'I mock you because you do not think. You should learn to engage your mind before you open your mouth.'

That, at least, shut her up for a while.

We crept along, keeping to the roadsides and ready to slip into a ditch or under the cover of the trees should anyone come riding past. One time, a cart clattered along, its boards splattered with half-festering fish. The man chewed a piece of straw, oblivious to the stench and to us as we crouched behind a thick tree trunk.

It was partly true, my reason for keeping out of sight: it was because of murder, and not just the one Luella thought would be taking place. I could not be seen as the sole companion of a girl who might be found dead. Besides, I hoped Frank would be gone after reading my note and that both Luella and I could slip away unnoticed as if we'd never been there at all.

Within an hour, Ulstone spread before us. It was a small village made up of one coaching inn and houses of old stone which lined the road that split through its middle. To the west, less than a mile away, the estuary spilled over the horizon, and at low tide, sand seemed to stretch to the end of the earth. To the east, the land was lush and framed by thick woodland where we now waited.

Set at the southern tip, a few feet off the roadside in its own patch of ground, was a single-storey brick building. To one side of it, a smithy was attached. The brickwork of the smithy was coarse, and where there might have been a door, there was just an opening, like a gaping mouth, that led inside. Horseshoes were nailed into the wooden frames which kept the building erect, and a hammer had been left carelessly outside.

Though I had never spent a single night within its walls, the place felt like home because Frank lived there. I could see him, hunched in the frame of that smithy, wearing his leather apron, blackened with soot, smiling at me. The image was only in my head of course. Nevertheless, there was a tingling in my chest, an excitement I never lost when I thought of being reunited with Frank, and Luella saw the smile which had spread over my face.

'This is it.' She came out from behind the tree and began to stride to the house. I caught her arm and dragged her back.

'Wait here. I will see if he is there.'

'I told you, Bonnie, you ain't leaving my side.'

I thought for a moment of punching her and knocking her out, but I did not have it within me. 'Stay close and off the road. We'll go in through the back. Don't let anyone see you.'

She was like my shadow as we scurried out of the covering of the trees and over the little stretch of field towards the side of the building. I had a sudden urge to laugh, for we must have looked so conspicuous to anyone who might have seen us that our espionage was surely pointless. Nonetheless, we pressed our bodies against the outside wall and tiptoed through some shrubbery until we came to a small, enclosed yard at the rear of the cottage. A heap of twigs lay haphazardly on the ground, a few buckets were filled with green rainwater, and a mangle had rusted from lack of use.

The back door did not fit in its frame, and it gave a

shudder as I pushed it open, grating against the floor tiles. The range had not been lit. There was a smell of damp woodsmoke, and when I crept into the front room, I saw that the grate held the ashen corpses of a few thin logs. The place was nothing more than a shell, and without pictures or paintings, rugs or blankets, there was nothing to give it comfort. There was only some wooden furniture and a few hard chairs, and in the bedroom, there was nothing but a single bed stuffed up at one end and a vast wooden chest. A jacket of his hung over one of the posts, and I kicked it under the bed out of sight.

'He's not here,' Luella said from the kitchen.

'It appears so.' He had received my note and had done as I had bid. My shoulders slid down from where they had been raised in fear; Frank was gone and safe. 'I shall check the smithy.'

I left her in the kitchen where she was stroking the table as if it were an animal.

Frank was not in the smithy. The coal fire was out, and the bricks of the chimney were cold.

'Not there,' I said somewhat breathlessly as I returned to her, for the relief was making me giddy. Luella had taken a seat on the kitchen bench; her arms rested on the tabletop, and her head hung low.

'Where is he, Bonnie?'

'I don't know. He's gone. None of his things are here.'

'What's in the chest?'

'What chest?'

'The chest in the bedroom.'

'How should I know?'

'It's locked.'

'Is it?' I rubbed my hands together, and they were cool and sticky. 'I think it must have come with the house. Probably something to do with the landlord.'

She raised her head, and her eyes were wider and bluer than ever. 'What do we do now?'

It was not yet midday. I had no need to rush. She needed consoling, and then I would be able to get her on her way.

'Fetch that firewood from outside, and we'll make some tea, shall we?'

She nodded and, in some sort of daze, did as she was told. There was a bucket to the side of the range with a few coals at the bottom, and after the wood had caught, she placed the coals on top. It was an old range, uncovered, and together we watched the flames grow stronger.

'There's a well not far, just by the road. I'll get some water.'

She did not object to my leaving this time, and I found her in the same place, still gazing at the fire, when I returned to hang the kettle over the heat. A corner in the kitchen acted as a larder, and inside there was a bunch of dirty carrots, a pot of flour and a pot of oats, some sprouting potatoes, and a tin of tea. I shut the door on it before she had time to see the food within.

'He's been here recently. I can smell him.'

On the side, there were a few chipped cups, and I laid them before us on the table. 'What do you mean, you can smell him?'

She was not looking at me. The crease was deep between her brows. 'Maybe he does,' she whispered to herself, and I was about to ask her what she was talking about when she faced me. 'Where is he, Bonnie?'

'I already said, I don't know.'

'You sent him a note.'

I laughed. 'I did not.' The kettle was steaming, and I used an old, stinking cloth to lift if off the heat and pour it into the teapot.

'You sent the landlord with it yesterday. I know you did. Did you tell Frank to go? Did you tell him we was close?'

'You are being ridiculous.' The cups ticked as the scalding water ran into them, and they threatened to crack.

'Then why is he not here?' Her voice rang in the quiet. She dipped her head as her tears spilled onto her cheeks, and she cradled herself.

Sipping my tea, I let my gaze fall through the window outside. A blue tit, with its black band over its eyes, flitted amongst the shrubbery and onto a branch of a silver birch which looked as if it had only been growing a few years. I sat there, the teacup burning my palms, listening to Luella sniff and dribble, and my eyelids began to droop. I could have rested my cheek on that tabletop and fallen asleep right then, I was sure, and not woken if a war had broken out.

'Maybe he's drinking,' Luella said. Wood scraped against tiles as she pushed out her bench and made for the door.

I caught her dress, and there was a terrible sound as the material ripped. It stopped us both. We stared at the gaping hole near her right hip, at the petticoat beneath.

'What've you done?' she whispered, before sobbing again and turning for the door.

I pushed it shut, placing myself between her and her escape. 'You cannot go out like that now; they will think you mad.'

She roared, grabbed my shoulders, and shoved me against the door. Her face came to within an inch of mine, and she bared her teeth. 'You will go to the inn, and you will bring him here.'

Once she had dropped me, I discovered, with a bark of laughter that bordered on hysteria, that I was shaking. Little Luella had actually frightened me!

I nodded, agreeing to what she asked, and left her at a sprint. Outside, I gulped the air and told myself what a fool I was being. I would go to the inn to please her, to placate her, but Frank would not be there.

Church bells rang clearly through the street. I was aware of the faces peering from the windows as I walked and of old men straightening their backs to stare at me as they weeded their front gardens. I held my head higher, pinched my gloves on tighter, and looked no one in the eye until I reached the inn.

The stagecoach driver had been and gone, so it seemed, for there were a couple of piles of steaming manure on the roadside. Inside, some men sat at the bar nursing beer in glass jugs, their shirtsleeves rolled up to their elbows, their shoes dusted with mud. All of them stared at me as I entered. Not one had the good grace to lower his eyes as I approached.

'Do any of you know where the blacksmith is?'

They glanced at each other until the youngest licked his lips and spoke. 'What do you want him for?'

'My horse needs a new shoe. Is he around?'

'Best go further on, love. Ain't seen him these last few days, and when I do, he's a workshy bastard.' The others sniggered into their beers, and the man grinned when he saw me blush.

'Right, thank you.' I turned for the door.

'Never knew him to be so popular with the ladies,' the man said to his friends.

'What do you mean?' I could not help my curiosity; I always was a jealous one. They found my interest amusing.

'A widow came in here a while back and saw him and seemed to like the look of him. Took her back with him to that palace of his.'

An older man blew bubbles in his beer as he laughed.

'A widow?'

The speaker nodded slowly as he looked me up and

down. 'Needed a bit of comforting, I expect. What's it to you anyway?'

'No. No, nothing. It's nothing to me.' I marched for the door and ignored him as he called, amidst a hail of laughter, if I too would not like to be comforted this afternoon.

I had reached Frank's cottage before I realised it. I had walked down the street seeing nothing, hearing nothing, feeling nothing, my mind blazing with who that widow might have been, what she might have looked like, how she might have made eyes at my Frank, and where they might have made love in that poky little place where every surface was skimmed with smuts. I gasped at the pain in my lip as I bit open a healing cut.

It had been months since I had seen Frank. He was a man, and hot blooded, and who could really trust a man? But it had never once occurred to me that he might take a lover. How stupid was I? For this was a village where strangers passed through all the time, the ideal place for indiscretions. How many might there have been, in all his years of living here, with me miles away making money for the both of us?

With my mind so full of fear and hatred and jealousy – and hope, for there was always a fleck of hope that the man at the inn had been nothing but a teaser – I had forgotten to plan what I would do with Luella. I reached the back door of the cottage and was about to enter when I heard a snatch of a conversation.

All fell silent as I opened the door. The kitchen was empty; they were in the other room. I could feel the buzzing of an energy and did not want to see what awaited me, but I pushed myself forward.

Luella cowered at the far end of the room. Frank was nearest to me, glaring at her. Both of them faced me as I entered.

Frank had grown fatter since I'd last seen him, and his

beard was longer than it had been. His skin had bronzed with the summer sunshine, and the lines around his eyes appeared ingrained with soot, so dark were they. He held the hammer that I had seen lying outside the smithy, his knuckles white from gripping it so tightly.

'Frank.' I smiled as widely as I could, though it pained me. I ran for him and kissed his cheek. 'This is Luella. She is a friend of mine from Stowmouth.' He frowned at me as if awaiting further explanation. 'We could not find you, so I went looking for you, and Luella stayed here. I hope you have not scared her.'

He dropped the hammer by his chair. 'Sorry – Luella? That right?'

His voice seemed strange to me – it had been so long since I had heard it that I had imagined it different in his absence. His Cumbrian accent was thick, and in that instant, I saw him as something like an ape, too big and animalistic and uncivilised, but just as soon as the thought came to me, I crushed it, embarrassed by my own snobbery.

'And you're from Stowmouth an' all?' He sat on his seat and picked the muck from under his fingernails, acting oblivious, acting as if her name had not been branded on to his skull.

'That's right.' Luella unfurled herself.

'Sorry to have scared you, Luella, only I don't get many visitors, and I thought you might've been coming to rob me.'

'That's all right.' She stared intently at the grate so that she didn't have to look at Frank. Perhaps her conscience was pricking her, for he had suddenly turned friendly and was smiling at her.

'Would you like any tea? Bonnie, would your friend like some tea?'

Luella fiddled with the chain about her neck. She was losing her nerve; I could see it. It was one thing to murder a stranger, but to murder someone after you'd sipped tea with them?

'Frank, could I speak with you outside?'

Both of them flicked their heads at me, but neither, not wanting to give up their secrets, objected when I led Frank into the yard and dragged him to the side of the house.

'What are you doing here? Did you not get my note?'

'I did, yes.' He was leaning against the wall, smirking as he brushed a curl of hair behind my ear.

'Then why are you not gone? I told you to wait on the beach for me.'

'Bonnie, the girl wants me dead, I can see it plain as day. You're too soft.' His smirk fell. 'We will stick to our plan.'

'I … I can't Frank. She is just a girl. She's … She is Samuel's daughter. I see him in her.'

'So?'

'I can't, Frank. Not after everything he –'

'He shouldn't mean anything to you.'

'He doesn't. But …'

'But what? What, Bonnie?'

'She is just a girl! She is scared, and she is hurt, that's all, but when she has healed, she'll forget all about us. If we go now, go to America like we've always dreamed about, she'll never find us.'

'I'll not be looking over my shoulder forever.'

'But you will have her death on your conscience. You are not a murderer, Frank.'

'No, I'm not.' He spat the words. I felt them stab into me.

The air shifted between us, grew taut. I backed away from him.

'The men at the inn said you had a woman here not long ago,' I said, trying to hurt him in return. 'A widow.'

He laughed and became very interested in the scenery beyond me.

'Is it true? You have been with other women?'

'They think me a single man. Other rumours would spread if I didn't take a girl now and again.'

He said it casually as if he had no idea of the force of the blow he had just delivered. I felt it in my gut, felt it knock the air out of me, and I staggered to the wall so that I did not fall to the ground. His attention remained fixed in the distance.

I glared at him and longed for the boy I had first seen when I was sixteen years old. The boy with the long limbs which never seemed under control, the boy who smiled when I smiled, the boy who held my hand and led me away into heaven with him.

'Didn't think you'd care anyway,' he said. 'Thought you'd be relieved, if anything.'

'How could you?'

He rolled his eyes to the sky. 'You've done the same to me.'

'Everything I've ever done has been for both of us. I did not take pleasure in any of it, and you know it!'

He sniggered, and it was just like the men at the bar that it made me want to heave.

'After all I have done for you. All the money I have made for you while you wait here, idle! They called you workshy, you know, at the inn. They called you workshy and lucky, and they were right. I have kept you, and you have grown fat and ugly on my work!'

'On your thieving, you mean?'

'Yes! You may laugh at me, Frank, for I surely am a fool. But I am more of a man than you have been these past few years.'

He had me by the throat before I knew it and hissed at me so that his spit flecked my face. 'I've been waiting, as you told me to. I've been ready, Bonnie. I could have gone years ago.'

'Then why didn't you? I know. Because you want as much money from me as you can get.'

'It is you who likes living like a lady, Bonnie! I would have been in America with you now if you'd had the guts to start afresh when we said we would. Do not blame me for your cowardice and greed. And do not speak to me like I am not your husband!'

After a shove, he let go of me, and I felt all the love between us dissipate into the air. This was why we lived so far apart: because we could no longer bear each other. Both of us loved the people we used to be before Bridgefield; neither of us could stand what we had become. We were stuck together not because of love, but because of our crimes.

He threw his head back, and his chest rose as he breathed in long and slow. 'We will stick to our plan.'

'I won't do it, Frank.'

'Then I shall tell her what really happened that night. Is that what you want?'

His scowling face blurred in my vision. I blinked, and a tear fell over my cheek. I shook my head.

'Then go and boil the kettle. Make us tea before she starts to suspect anything.'

I did as he said, shivering as he followed me inside.

'TEA, LUELLA?' I set the kettle over the fire again and arranged the cups again, though now my hands would not cease their shaking. Frank leaned against the back door watching me.

'Put my case in the bedroom will you, dear?'

Reluctantly, he took my bag from where it had been lying on the kitchen floor and passed Luella at the entrance to the bedroom. Out of the corner of my eye, I saw them hesitate beside each other.

I made myself busy, tidying things that were already tidy. I wiped the top of the table, feeling crumbs under my hands that I had not seen before. I threw out the old tea leaves from the pot. I washed the sink clean of coal smears.

'What is that tune?' Luella said.

I was so on edge that I hadn't realised I'd been humming. 'Oh, just something my mother used to sing.'

'My ma too.'

Our eyes met. Suddenly, it was as if there was a gaping chasm between us; we were both too far gone in our plans to save each other, but oh, how we wished we could have stopped everything right then! Tears stung my eyes as I struggled to smile.

'Do you know the words?'

'It's about a baby,' Luella said. 'Rock a bye baby on the treetop ...'

The image of my mother peering over me, a bottle of gin and a spoon in her hand to shut me up, her lips forming those words which were laced with a hidden threat ... I couldn't bear to hear any more.

'Funny how you forget the details of things,' I said, cutting her off.

The moment between us was lost. The kettle's spout was steaming.

'Time for tea.'

I felt the heat of her through my dress as she watched me pour. Frank was somewhere behind us in one of the other rooms though I was aware that he could sneak up on anybody easily.

'Where's your flask?' Luella whispered. Her white fingers fluttered to a cup, then back to her chest.

'In my case.'

'Go and get it then.'

Trying to keep my footsteps light and regular, I made my way to the bedroom. Frank was not there; he must have been in the front room. My case lay on the bed, unopened, and my fingers were so stiff that it was a task to undo the clasps, and as one flicked open, it cut my flesh. I did not feel the pain of it, only saw the slice start to seep with red until it was as if there was a rosehip at the end of my finger. I watched it grow and grow until the weight of it was too much, and it fell off my finger and dropped onto Miss Grey's silver salter. The splatter of blood shocked me. I sucked at my wound and quickly grabbed the flask without another glance at all the stolen goods amidst my silk dresses.

In the kitchen, Luella stared at the three cups. A raindrop crashed into the window and startled us both, and for a moment we watched as water fell as big as buttons from the sky.

'This is yours.' Luella moved the cup that I had drunk from before nearer to me. 'Which one for Frank?'

The other two were clean; Luella had not drunk any tea earlier. Both were quite similar in appearance with blue paintwork that had once looked dainty and grand but had faded from so much use. I pointed at the one on the right and handed her the flask.

She opened it slowly as if death would spring out and take her if she disturbed it too much. The arsenic came out the same colour as the tea and mixed well. She sniffed it and gestured that I do the same. No one would ever have known it was poison.

'Half a cup won't be enough,' I said, though I didn't know why I was bothering; the amount would surely end a small girl like Luella, which was the point. My mouth was running away, trying to fill the silence in my panic. 'He'd need all of it to kill him.'

'Then we'll make another pot after this one.'

She turned to put the kettle on the hook. As she did so, I picked up my cup and the one free of poison and said as she was returning, 'I best give it to him. He'll think it strange if you serve him.'

She nodded, and time slowed as she took that blue-rimmed cup in her tiny fingers. She urged me forwards, keen to see her revenge unfold, and I knew, with a dreadful sickness, that the last thing she would ever see would be the faces of the people who had ruined her life.

I walked, as one does in dreams, as if through water. I gave Frank his tea and took the seat beside him. My face felt strange, and I touched my fingers to it and found that the corners of my lips were lifted; I was smiling.

'A nice cup of tea,' Frank said, slurping it up. He prodded me with his elbow, and I sipped the drink.

'It's hot. Be careful,' I said, to neither of them in particular, and I don't know why I said it for it was not hot at all, it was almost cold, in fact. I was just trying to fill the silence.

'So, Luella, what's it that you do down by the seaside? You got a nice old mistress to take care of like Bonnie does?'

The conversation swirled around me. How I wished to shut Frank's mouth; I would have taken a needle and sewn it tight if I could have. It was not enough to kill her; he had to mock her too.

'That's right.' Luella's voice sounded a long way off in the corner of the room.

There was more silence. I drank again.

'Do you know a place called Bridgefield? It's not too far from here.' Frank was playing with her, throwing embers at her and seeing if they would catch. 'We used to work there, didn't we, Bonnie? Nice place, though Bonnie didn't get on too well with the man of the house.'

'Frank.' My tongue was thick as I talked. 'Luella doesn't want to hear it.'

'You are friends, are you not? Same line of work. I'm sure Luella's had her fair share of nosy old men, finding things out they shouldn't.'

'Frank!'

I did not know who he was trying to torture more: me or Luella. I dragged my eyes upwards, and they took a while to focus, but when they did, Luella was glaring at me, her cup still full in her hands, the liquid rippling as she quaked. It was the same kind of stare as when I'd first seen her on the green outside Miss Grey's house, that same intensity, and it brought that day back to me.

Monday … My first thought. Monday and fair of face …

How had I not asked? All these days together, never knowing …

'Luella.' My lips moved before the sound came. I drank some more. 'What day were you born?'

The question surprised her. 'Not sure.' Her voice was slowing; was that the poison? 'I think Thursday … Thursday seems familiar.'

'Thursday.' I laughed a little. I was starting to feel rather giddy, and my head was becoming lighter on my shoulders. 'I would never have said Thursday.' I laughed again, and the sound was peculiar. My hand was cool as I felt the pulse in my neck, and I wondered at how slow it seemed. 'Far to go … Thursday's child has far to go.'

'That's right. Drink your tea now.' Frank pushed the cup to my lips and tilted it so that the tea swamped my mouth, and I had no choice but to swallow. I swallowed and swallowed until all of it was gone.

My lips were wet. The air on them was cold. I lifted my hand to wipe them with my sleeve, but nothing happened.

My hand would not move. I stared down at my body, so still and calm.

Thoughts came and went from my mind. It was like a blanket had been thrown over me, and I was descending lower and lower. The blanket was muffling everything, making the room around me grow dark, making me feel warm and safe and glowing, though somewhere in the pit of my stomach there was a panic.

I forced through the fog in my head and pushed my eyelids wide. To my left, Frank. To my right, Luella. Both with full teacups. Both staring at me, waiting.

In the darkness, the last thing I heard was my cup smashing on the tiles as it fell from my hand.

PART II

LUELLA

CHAPTER 7

The thing about Bonnie were that she thought everything were all about her. It were, I suppose. This were all about her, right from the beginning.

THERE'S no use starting from where we've left off. You wouldn't understand. You'd think me mean, double-crossing, maybe a whore. I were all of them things in a way.

Where should I start? The death of my pa? That's just a small thing to me now, so I'll tell that later. When I first saw Bonnie? I think that will wait. The murder of Mr Campbell? But he meant nothing to me, even though it were at the heart of all this.

I'll start less than two weeks before Bonnie drank that tea. I'll start at the start of August in the year of 1865. It'd been eight years and one day since Pa's killing, and I were outside Grandma's cottage with my arms deep in water, rinsing the laundry in the early morning, when a boy ran up and threw a letter at me and scarpered before I'd had chance to get my hands dry.

They all did that; ran to us, all the way out there by the woods, and then they ran away from us quicker. I were the daughter of a murderer, see. I couldn't be trusted. Though they trusted us with their dirty sheets and their drawers with shit stains in them.

I took up the letter off the stone wall.

The paper were fair enough. The handwriting were neat, but there weren't much of it. The person what wrote it didn't think it worth including the details. Who needed details anyway when they was told their own ma were dead and had done it herself?

Grandma heard the silence and knew I weren't working. It were that what drew her out away from her ironing, all red-faced and glaring like usual. She held her tongue when she saw the state of me, though. I weren't crying. I'd say it were shock, but that'd be a fib too. It were just a sort of numbness and, deep, deep down, something like a tight ball of fire what I'd not felt burn for some time.

She took the letter from me, but we both knew she didn't understand it.

'Ma's dead.'

Something passed over her face, like a grimace, as if she might have had a heart after all. She folded the letter.

'Right.'

She went inside, dipping to fit under the doorway, and left me standing there with the sun on my shoulders.

If the letter came that day, Ma probably finished herself the day before. The anniversary – at least it wouldn't be trouble for me to remember. I were thinking this as I walked inside the cottage. I could only see the fire burning until my eyes got used to the dark. Then I saw the irons what was facing the flames, cooking nicely, and the shirt what was on the table, steaming and setting. Grandma were in the next room where we slept. I heard her sniffing and the paper crackling in her hands.

'I'll go then,' I said, and then she came through. Her eyes didn't look wet. She threw the letter on the fire before I could catch it.

'Be damned.'

I thought she were saying that about Ma, not me, but I couldn't be sure.

'You ain't going.'

'Who will get her things?'

'Leave them. They'll sell them or burn them.'

I thought of Ma's things in a furnace, the last of her going to nothing but dust, and I couldn't bear it.

In the next room, there were a trunk. The bits from our house – mine, Ma's, and Pa's before everything went wrong – were in there. There weren't much. Anything what had been worth anything were sold long ago, except for the dress. It had been full of muck and silt last time it had seen daylight, but it were good enough; Grandma had washed it well. We'd kept it in case I ever needed it, and now I did.

Grandma didn't help me get it on. Ma died three years ago to her, and she didn't wear black then. She stood in the doorway with her arms folded, scowling at me.

'Stubborn. Your father's daughter,' she said now and then as I struggled to do the buttons on my back.

We'd no black hat. I wore my straw bonnet like always and it looked right out of place, but better to have a covered head than nothing at all. I'd no gloves neither. The black showed up the red cracks on my white skin, and a thought passed me: at least it would be a day away from the wash bucket.

A day away from the wash bucket! Going to see the corpse of my ma – a holiday!

Grandma were still huffing and puffing at me. How

would she cope? We'd got a big load to do. Did I see the burn on her wrist? That were from rushing already. Her fingers was too stiff to be working in water all day.

I'd long stopped listening to her. I didn't say nothing as I took the pennies off the windowsill – the ones which was mine – and grabbed my bag what I'd had since I was a little 'un and walked out the cottage. I walked a good twenty feet and wondered if Grandma were watching and cursing me, but when I turned round, the doorway were empty.

I walked down to the lane and kept going until the buildings came into view. Bridgefield. Home. Hell.

It were busy with women and maids out shopping. All of them turned at me, thinking me someone new to the place, and then dropped their mouths like dead fishes when they recognised me. They hadn't seen me in black for years. I guessed they knew why I were wearing it now, and not one of them approached to offer their condolences.

I didn't look at them. I kept walking. I went straight through the high street. The smell were ripe because of the sun, and although I hated that cottage I had to call home, I hated the stench of Bridgefield town even more where pigs rotted as they hung on their hooks and vegetables turned to slime on the kerbsides.

I walked all the way down the hill and saw the river. It were low. The island in the middle of it below the bridge were showing (it's flooded most other times of the year), and there was ducks on it. I crossed the bridge and glanced once at the water and felt the cold of it on me, and my head got dizzy at the memory, so I turned my gaze to the paving stones.

On the other side of the bridge, a quarter of a mile downriver, were the carpet factory belching out noise and stench. I turned my back on it and followed the road out of Bridgefield, heading east, and as I walked, I felt myself get lighter and also crushed.

My ma were dead.

She'd been away so long it were like she'd been dead for a while anyway. But I always knew, at the back of my mind, that she were somewhere nice. I used to think of her sitting in one of them window seats looking over the gardens and the city and hoped it would take her mind off things. I used to think of her eating roast beef when we had nothing but bread for breakfast, dinner, and supper. I used to think of joining her for a while, pretending. It wouldn't have taken much to be admitted; I could've faked it. I'd rather've been with the lunatics than my own grandma most days, but I'd lost my nerve.

I walked until I were on the main road, and then I sat under the shade of a tree. A stagecoach would be coming by sometime. Better a stagecoach than a train. Never liked trains. Pa used to like trains; we'd have whole days on them. I couldn't hear them hoot nor see their steam without thinking of Pa and that smile of his, the way he wrapped his hand around Ma's waist as the train set off, and the way he rubbed the top of my head all excited as if we was the only things he'd ever need.

I would not set foot on a train for as long as I lived.

So I waited.

I were at the asylum before teatime.

I HAD to walk to the building from the city centre. I saw it looming, all grand and big at the top of the hill. It were a pretty place; who'd have thought lunatics would need such nice surroundings? It were supposed to help, so I were led to believe. The fresh air. The views. Digging up spuds. Keeping your bed tidy. Pruning the bushes. Washing and ironing. It were supposed to calm you, and that were what most lunatics needed: calming.

Didn't do my ma no good.

There were an avenue of trees. I couldn't name them. They had thin trunks and apple-green leaves and stood up properly without slouching. They blocked my view of the asylum as I walked through the middle of them, and when I came out from between them, I were at the foot of a short drive and facing me were a great big wooden door and so many windows! The windows shocked me. Like unblinking eyes in the building's face, they was, and I wondered who might have been watching me from behind them.

Around me, I could hear the lunatics working in the gardens, though I couldn't see them. The sound of my own shoes bounced off the trees as I walked up to the door and were allowed inside.

The smell of cleaning and carbolic hit me. I were led down one of them long corridors. Rooms broke off from the corridor, but I couldn't see what were in the rooms because the doors was heavy and locked. I heard voices though, the odd cry and screech, and I kept close to the woman in the uniform what were walking too fast in front of me.

I couldn't say which way she took me. I don't know how anybody found their way around that place and through all them doors what needed unlocking and locking again so that there were the constant jingle of keys as the woman fiddled with her set on a great iron ring. I wondered how my ma had found the place when she were here, if she'd ever known there were an administrative block where the attendants and the superintendent slept, or that there were a dead room somewhere, waiting for her arrival.

The dead room came up on us quick. I were just getting used to the endless march, and the nervousness had left my stomach – I thought we'd never find Ma and that I wouldn't have to see her and wouldn't have to believe that she were really gone – when suddenly the next door opened into a room what were cold and small and fair on dark but for the high windows.

And there she were. On an old table with an old shroud to cover her. There were a bowl, a jug of water – cold, so I were to find out – and a cloth so that I could wash her. For a moment, I didn't move. I couldn't go to her and see what she had become. I wanted to run out of there, and I thought I'd smash through the locks if I had to, just to get some air.

'Have you money for a burial?' the attendant asked. It were the only thing she'd said to me, and her voice were kind compared to the look of her.

I shook my head.

'Pauper's it'll be then.' She touched me on the shoulder because I'd started to weep.

'Can I go to it?'

'It'll be at night, what with her ... you know.' Killing herself, she meant to say.

'They won't take her, will they? The doctors. They won't cut her up?' Like they'd done with Pa's body. The body of a murderer, a man in his prime; they couldn't wait to hack him down. It hadn't seemed too bad for Pa to be cut, but Ma! So small and thin and pretty. I couldn't bear for them to slice into her lovely skin.

'We'll get her in the parish,' the woman said, but she said it in a way what sounded like she couldn't be certain of her own promise.

She left me then, and when the door shut, I were sure she'd locked me in, and I couldn't get my breath for a while. I had to put my head between my knees and breathe slow before I could walk to Ma.

She'd changed since I'd last seen her. She looked healthier now than she had done when she'd first come here. The hollows of her cheeks had plumped out, and though her skin were grey with death, it were clear, and I thought it must have been pearly before she'd taken herself.

Her hair were plaited close to her scalp, and the ends was fixed up on to her head; I were grateful that she hadn't been shorn. There were a little pair of blunt scissors by the wash things, and I cut out them ties and let her hair fall free. She had such lovely hair. Nicer than mine because it were so smooth. I cut a few inches off it and brushed it against my cheek, knotted it, and placed it in my bag so I could keep a bit of her with me always. And then I set about washing her.

You'd have thought nothing were wrong with her. Not a bruise on her skin, not a blemish. Just as beautiful as I'd always remembered her. You'd have thought she'd have died peaceful in her sleep, taken by the Lord because she'd asked so nicely, until you got to her wrists. They was bandaged, but the blood had come through, and when I looked more closely – it were hard to see in the dimness – I could make out the brown marks on her hands and arms and some smudges on her face where the blood had dried on, though the attendants had tried to wipe most of it off. I scrubbed her hands and cleaned her nails until I were fair on sweating, and when I'd finished, I hid her arms under the shroud so that none of the violence she'd done to herself showed; she were just a pretty head at the top of a white shroud with pretty hair splayed around her face like she could've been an angel.

The door opened then, and I wondered if there were some kind of peephole that the woman could see through. She waited just inside the room for me.

'How did she do it?'

The attendant cleared her throat. I don't think she wanted to say, but I waited until she did. 'A fork. Took it from the dining room. Hid it up her sleeve.'

She'd told me about them forks in the one letter she'd

sent me when she'd first arrived. They was webbed most of the way up, she'd said; just the very tips of them was like a proper fork, and she couldn't get used to eating with them. She must have used some force. What a state she must have been in under them bandages!

The thought made my vision go dark. I leaned over Ma, looking only at her face, and kissed her cold forehead. Then I walked out that room and left my ma forever.

I didn't notice the locks this time, nor the voices from the other side of the doors. I watched the woman's rubber shoes on the black-and-white tiled floor and focused on my breathing until suddenly we was in the administrative block again and she were handing me a box with Ma's things in it.

The box lid were dusty. The last time someone's hands had been on it must have been three years ago when Ma arrived, when her things still held a bit of her warmth.

They was cold now. They smelt as if they'd been locked away for too long – that musky kind of smell, a bit damp. There weren't much. A pair of old shoes, but they was no use because Ma's feet was much smaller than mine and Grandma's, so I gave them to the attendant and said she could do what she liked with them. There were a bonnet and some hair pins, and the bonnet were better than the one I were wearing, so I decided to keep that. There were the dress what she'd been brought in wearing, and as I sniffed it, I were sure it smelt of her, of her skin and sweat as well as carbolic – that were from the washing she'd done at Grandma's. It were an old dress, one from her youth what had been her favourite, the one she'd met my pa in, so the story went. The attendant looked at me all hopeful, but I folded it up small and neat and put it in my bag.

Only two things remained in the box: a locket on a chain what was rusted and a handkerchief. I prised open the locket and saw my pa's likeness smiling at me, and I shut it quick.

The handkerchief were Pa's too, and Ma had always kept it hidden in her bodice next to her heart after he died, so I couldn't get rid of that neither.

I thanked the attendant, and I didn't ask any other questions about what would happen to Ma's body. I didn't want any letters about it neither. I could imagine her in a nice spot in a peaceful churchyard that way, not in the middle of twelve other paupers, their juices running all over her or, worse, on a doctor's slab with her flesh flayed off the bones surrounded by toffs and scalpels.

I left the asylum and shuddered when that great big door shut me out. Better that though than shut me inside. How stupid I'd been to think I'd like to live in there rather than be free, whatever free meant.

I walked through the avenue of trees as the sun slanted low in the sky. I felt the distance grow between me and Ma but didn't feel sad. That weren't Ma in there, in that dead room; it were just her body. I had her with me here, in her hair and her clothes and that locket. I were carrying her away with me to freedom.

I had to hurry to get a coach because I weren't going to spend a night in Bristol. And so it were, when I were squashed beside a fat woman whose crinoline cut into my legs, that I opened my bag and took a real good look at Ma's things.

I put Ma's knot of hair in the locket so that it covered Pa's face and fastened it about my neck. And then my gaze fell on the handkerchief. The last time I'd seen it had been eight years ago after Grandma had cleaned it. I remembered how Ma had cursed her for it because it no longer smelt of Pa. I'd forgotten it, tell the truth.

I held it now between my fingers and felt the softness of it, the quality of it, remembering the boot marks on it after Pa's arrest. And something caught on my fingers – a ripple of silk thread. In the corner, a small, neat embroidery: *Samuel Blyth*. Beautifully done, a real work of art.

I had to put my hand to my mouth because I were scared I'd be sick.

A rage came over me. I think I yelled. I know the woman next to me got off at the next stop very quick, and there was some whisperings about whether I should be allowed to stay on board. The driver let me, though, and it were falling to dusk when I realised that I could not go back to Bridgefield, not yet. If I saw Grandma, I think I might've killed her.

So I stopped some miles before home in a place I'd never heard of before. A place not far from the channel what had an inn where I could buy some food and perhaps a bed for the night if my money stretched that far. A place where I could rage about my ma's death and everything before that. A place where I could plan out what I would do next as I drank too much beer. A place where I decided the only thing I needed now were revenge. A place where revenge came to me as easy as sleep to a drunkard.

Ulstone.

CHAPTER 8

And so I found myself sat in the corner of the public house, a pint of beer between my hands, a pain growing behind my eyes, and thinking of all them years ago. It kept coming to me, all the little bits, all in flashes. I couldn't put it straight, the timeline, I mean. When did that happen? Were that before or after?

Eight years. Almost half my life. And it did seem like a lifetime ago, like one of them times you ain't sure if it'd been real or if it'd been a dream. I couldn't feel Pa no more. I could barely remember the look of him. I remembered his woollen trousers and his boots what he always polished himself and took great pride in. I remembered him by his books, by his pointy pencil what he'd used to sharpen with his flick knife. I remembered the time he'd taught me to read – he must have tutored me lots of times, but they all merged into one – and his arm against mine and his fingers what was long and white as he'd showed me how to hold a pen. And how he'd give me sums, and said things like, if you had three shillings and bought an apple for one shilling, how much would you have left and how would you write that in this book of mine?

I remembered that teaching because it alarmed me – only one apple for a whole shilling!

The more I tried to remember – the more I tried to work things out – the worse the pain in my head got. I felt the locket around me like a ball and chain, and I opened it and looked again at Ma's hair and sniffed it and thought, you was right! But there were more to it than she'd ever known. I'd pushed my knowledge away; over the years, I'd been convinced through one way or another that I'd got it all wrong. I'd been weak. I'd hidden in that old cottage doing Grandma's bidding, believing everyone else but myself.

'I'll prove us right,' I said to the locket in a whisper, and then I heard laughter around me.

The men in the pub was looking at me. Very odd for a girl to be in a pub all on her own. I hadn't known if they'd serve me, but my money had proved just as good as anyone's. It hadn't bought privacy though.

A group of them was sat by the bar, turned so they was half facing me. Lord knows how long they'd been staring; I hadn't been taking no notice of them. And now I wished I hadn't caught their eye because they started talking at me – sort of talking at me and sort of talking between themselves about what they'd like to do with me.

One of them came over, a young man, not maybe ten years older than me. He sat on a stool beside me and belched and smirked. He smelt of sweat and cow shit.

'What you doing all on your own?'

I didn't answer him, just looked at my beer.

'Mourning someone?'

'Husband,' I said, and I don't know why I said that, but it just seemed easier than saying my ma and having to explain everything.

'Young to be a widow,' the man said and came closer.

'I'd like to be on my own, thank you.' He laughed at that,

and I have to admit it did sound a bit toity, even to my own ears.

'Wants to be on her own, lads,' he said over his shoulder, and they all laughed. 'I'd say she's come to the wrong place.'

'Let her alone, Stanley,' one of the men said, and I couldn't see him because he'd got his back to me. He'd been the only one what hadn't been staring.

Stanley laughed meanly. He stood up away from his stool and staggered over to the man.

'Ain't you the gent, Frank.'

Maybe it were because I'd been thinking of the memories. Maybe if Ma hadn't just died and if I hadn't seen what I'd seen on the handkerchief, I might never have thought of it. But the name Frank struck me like a punch in the face. I remembered the man at Mrs Campbell's, the big man, the outside man, what'd had dark hair like Pa but were much grubbier. I looked now at this man at the bar. He'd turned towards Stanley, and I could see half his face. It were creased like old leather and fair on brown, and his hair were dark and curly. There must have been lots of country men what looked sun-beaten and dirty, and plenty what was called Frank too, but there were just something about him ...

'Let the lass be. You're making a fool of yourself.'

It were the voice, the accent. The man at Mrs Campbell's had been quiet, and I'd only ever really heard him talk to the animals. I'd gone over to visit Mrs Campbell in late spring because she'd got herself a new donkey, because the donkeys was my favourite. I'd gone to say hello to it, and that Frank had been there and he'd told me the donkey's name and that he were a cheeky one because he'd already had a bite out of him that morning. I couldn't understand some of the things he'd said because of his accent. Later, Mrs Campbell had told me, when she'd poured me some lemonade she'd made herself that afternoon, that Frank were from the north, a place called Cumbria, where they speaks different from us down here.

Now, there wasn't many folks what I'd heard in all them eight years since Pa's death what spoke like that, except this one here before me, and his name too being Frank ... well, for a moment I felt as if I couldn't move.

I watched with my mouth open as Frank and Stanley squared up to each other, calling each other names, and the men around them rubbed their hands on their thighs as if they was about to see a cockfight. Frank turned towards me, and I saw then that it really were him after all these years, aged a bit but still recognisable, here in Ulstone, not thirty miles from Bridgefield! He saw me gawping at him and no doubt took it that I thought him some kind of shining knight, and he winked at me and then thumped Stanley clear in the mouth. Stanley tumbled back, and the landlord behind the bar raised his voice and said that were enough of that sort of thing. Stanley grunted and growled for a bit but limped off to his pint of beer, holding his bleeding lip. Frank threw back whatever were left of his beer, keeping his eyes on me as he lifted up his glass, then made his way to the door.

'Wait!'

All of the men turned to me. Frank's hand were on the knob, but he stopped and grinned as if he'd known all along that I could never resist him.

'Want to take some air, miss?' he said, and opened the door and waited for me.

My plate and cutlery was still on my table from the eggs I'd ate earlier. Frank smirked at the men what was whispering amongst themselves, and I took that time to slip the fork – what was certainly sharper than any asylum fork – up my sleeve. Not looking at the men what was no doubt calling me a whore, I followed Frank outside.

'WHERE'VE YOU COME FROM?' he said. We was walking down the little road with the houses around us. The sun had gone to bed for the night, and the stars was out and the moon were bright. It were a beautiful night; not the kind of night for a killing.

'Bristol.' It weren't really a lie.

'When did your man die?'

'Not long ago.'

'Sorry.' But he didn't sound it; he sounded eager, and he started to walk faster.

I started to worry then because I'd seen him smack that Stanley and it'd looked like he'd only swatted a fly. And here I were with a little bent fork up my arm. Maybe I could have poked him in the eye with it.

'Where we going?' I said, because I didn't think any proper widow would have just gone walking off with a strange man what she'd never met before and not ask any questions, but I couldn't be sure; I'd never known a 'proper' widow.

'Back to mine for a drink. I've whiskey, if you like it.'

'Ain't never had whiskey before.'

'Then I think you'll like it.'

I followed him, and all the while the rage in me were building. Here he were, cocksure and without a care in the world as my ma were most likely being thrown into a pauper grave without a prayer said over her.

I'd seen him that night, you see. Eight years ago. I'd seen him as I'd been hiding in the gardens. I'd seen him run, his arms filled with all his things, and his face white and scared and full of guilt. He'd run, and under the light of the moon, he'd looked just like a spirit whisping away into the darkness.

He'd never come back. No one even asked for him, which

I'd never understood. He vanished just as quickly as he'd come, as if he'd never been there. I suppose it were because he were just a labourer. He slept outside in the barn. He worked well and quietly and never caused a fuss. For such a big man, he'd known how to make himself invisible, while Bonnie did her best to make sure everyone saw her.

Frank led me towards the end of the village and stopped at a run-down little place. I don't know why I thought it run-down; Grandma's cottage had a dirt floor and two rooms and that were it, but I always compared things to my real home what we'd lived in before. This place smelt of metal and coal and heat and dirt; it smelt of Frank. He took me in through the back door, and the fire were low but burning in the kitchen, but he didn't stop in there. He went straight through to the front room and put a cushion on one of the hard chairs for me and told me to sit and he'd just go and fetch that whiskey.

I heard him pouring it in the kitchen, and I slipped the fork out my sleeve a little and had it ready in my hand but so that he couldn't see it. When he came back, I took the glass of whiskey in my other hand. He watched to see what I'd make of the drink and seemed disappointed when I didn't pull a face at the strength of it; I'd had a fair share of gin in my time so that whiskey didn't burn.

'Why've you come here, miss? You don't know me; I don't know you.'

'Wanted some company.'

He leaned forward and rested his elbows on his thighs. 'I'd believe that if you didn't look so angry. You should know that it doesn't suit you to scowl.'

'You think I care if you like my face or not?'

He rested back and downed his drink. 'Oh, I like the look of you very much.'

I'd never had a man say such a thing to me. I'd thought

myself ugly all my life; I used to believe Pa when he'd called me pretty, but ever since what happened, I'd come to think everything he'd ever said had been nothing but lies. And all the boys in town would tease and taunt me, if ever they caught me on my own, and try to pull my hair to see if I'd come after them with a knife. I'd recognised fear in folk's faces, pity sometimes, curiosity, but never lust. Grandma had warned me about men, tried to scare me so that I'd never leave her and her cottage. It were her warnings what I heard in my head as Frank continued to look me all over, and I felt myself flushing.

'What's your name?' he said.

'Why do you want it?'

He smiled and shrugged. 'Are you planning on staying the night here, Miss Someone? Or shall you be going in a minute?'

He twisted his empty glass in his great big hands. I'd seen him down a fair few pints and that whiskey, but he weren't much altered by any of it yet. I were though, so I stopped myself from drinking any more because I'd need to be sharp if I were going to do anything tonight.

'I'm staying.'

His lips spread over all his teeth in a grin, and he got up from his chair and moved towards me.

'More whiskey,' I said, to stop him in his tracks.

And sure enough, he went to the kitchen and came back to top up my glass and poured himself a measure what reached all the way to the rim of his glass. I toasted the night with him. He gulped it all and then poured himself another. Somehow I made sure my face stopped scowling and started to smile instead. He really did think himself in for a nice treat.

IT TOOK a few more glasses before he went drowsy. He squinted at me, as if I were too far away, then tugged me closer. He sat me down on his knee, and his hands was all over my legs. I went very still. I'd had no one touch me in years, let alone ever touch me like that. He didn't seem to notice though, and he pulled on my hair to bring my lips to his.

It were awful. His breath were ripe with whiskey, his lips all dry and rough, and then his tongue! Too hot and slimy; I thought of it like an eel popping out, all alive and wriggling, and I had to break away from him quick.

He must've thought that were a good thing because he were up on his feet in a flash and were guiding me towards another door what I hadn't been through before. Once it opened, I saw the bed in the corner, and then I really started to panic.

He got me against the wall. I had the fork up my sleeve but couldn't get it out without him noticing, and truth be told, I didn't seem to know where I ended and he started. It were all limbs and hair and mouths and heavy breathing and his hands pressing into me in places what made me squirm.

I were in this tangle when another memory came back to me. I'd been playing in the barn with the new kittens. I were at the top of a mound of hay when there were a shuffling sound below. I peeked over and there were Frank and a lady, but I couldn't see her properly for the angle of it. They was kissing and she were laughing, and I thought the laugh seemed familiar because it sounded fake like she didn't really mean it, and there were only one other woman what I knew what sounded like that: Mrs Campbell's new companion. They was muffling words to each other, and there were the sound of something like metal catching on a fingernail, then more laughter, and then it went quiet. That's when they was kissing. That's when I saw her face turn my way a little, and it definitely were Mrs Campbell's companion, Bonnie. It were such a strange sight because Bonnie were always so neat and smart, and she spoke all proper and posh as if she might've come from London. Frank were the last person I'd ever have thought she'd have been with like that.

And then it all got a bit more serious. There was no more giggles. Their breath came quick, and he must have shoved her against one of them beams because I heard her thump into it, and it must have hurt but she didn't say nothing. His head went down onto her chest as she tilted hers back and closed her eyes. But then she started shaking her head a little. He were trying to bring up her skirts, but then she really started saying no, no, that he mustn't, that he should stop. Stop! She pushed him off her, and I'd never seen a face so full of anger as Frank's then. He turned away from her and did something with himself in his trousers, and Bonnie just stood there real still.

I must have been holding on to a little kitten during all that, and them kittens was as feral as their mother, and it didn't want me to be touching it no more so it bit me. I didn't scream but I must have gasped because Bonnie's head snapped up in my direction. I think I'd hid myself quite well though. She didn't call me down or say nothing to Frank; I just heard her heels clipping outside and heading back for the house, and then I heard Frank call her a bitch.

All this flashed through my mind in a few seconds as Frank were kissing my neck and unbuttoning my dress. In that instant I knew – they'd been in on it together! Of course ... the handkerchief, him running into the night all guilty-like ...

It made me feel so sick – to be touched by a murderer! While he were down by my neck, kissing it, I took a gulp of air and shoved him so hard that he went toppling back. He twisted, trying to right himself, but there were a chest in the room, and he tripped on that. I heard his kneecap smash on the floor tiles as he fell to the ground. He didn't know what were happening, and in a moment I were on his back, my legs wrapped round him as he tried to shake me off, and I were thumping and punching and slapping him, and riding him like he were some kind of unbroken pony.

And God, it felt good!

My screams was screeching all around me. My hair were getting in my face, but I couldn't brush it back because my hands was too concerned with striking Frank. He were cursing as I ripped out clumps of his hair and raked my nails over his neck until it were bleeding. In all the commotion, I heard him asking what in hell's name I were doing (there was more curse words in it than that), and I were so high on the violence, on the blood, and on the pain I were causing that I think I might have laughed.

'Frank Adams,' I shouted, panting and struggling. 'Frank Adams. Murderer! Don't you remember me? Don't you remember the Blyths?'

I'd grown a bit weak by that point – my arms was starting to ache – so I tugged out the fork and I were ready to stab it into his neck. I were thirsty for it, to see all his blood spill out on the ground as he realised they hadn't got away with it after all, but as I were getting the fork ready, I found myself flying, my feet off the ground.

I came down on the bed, which were probably for the best as even that felt like stone as I hit it. Something went crack, and later I realised that must have been my head against the wall because I had a huge lump there in the morning. Then Frank were hobbling towards me like a proper old gargoyle, and though there were a little blood trickling from the back of his neck onto his collar, the rest of him looked as if I'd not done anything but give him a bit of a ruffling.

He were too quick – or I were too slow – and he were on top of me before I could do a thing. His weight pressed down on the tops of my legs as he sat over me, and still I tried scratching at him. The prongs of the fork clawed close enough to his face that he jerked back in fright, and with a growl, he punched that fork right out of my hand. It skidded across the floor too far away for me to reach.

He were going to kill me. I could see it as I lay there underneath him. His face were red and shiny, and some of the veins was raised so that I could see his pulse twitching under the skin of his forehead. What a fool I'd been! Coming here with him like this with nothing but a fork and my anger and stupidity. All them years of thinking of how I'd save Ma, how I'd make it all right, how I'd put everything straight. And now I were just a weak little girl about to be murdered.

I started to cry. I hated myself for it, but I couldn't stop it. I wanted my ma. I wanted Mrs Campbell. Hell, I would have been happy with Grandma! I wanted everything to go back to how it had been before, when Ma used to sing as she watered her pot plants in the parlour, when Pa used to kiss her and take me on his knee, when Mrs Campbell used to brush my hair and tell me how she wished she'd had a daughter like me.

I searched for the locket around my neck, held it close, and wept on it. I had my ma with me now, I tried to tell myself. I had her in that locket. And really, what were there to live for? If Frank finished me, I would be with Ma and Pa and Mrs Campbell; I'd meet them in heaven and spend eternity beside them. My tears turned from fear to longing. I went limp. I were ready for the pain that there surely must be in dying.

BUT FRANK just sat on top of me, frowning. He got his breath back and wiped a bit of blood off his neck.

I were still sobbing. It were like something had broken inside me, and all of me were tumbling out. I couldn't stop it. It kept coming and coming and coming, getting stronger, until it were strangling me. For a moment, I thought Frank had his hands about my neck, but when I touched myself there were nothing but my own skin.

I were dying.

Frank's weight lifted off me, the mattress moved a bit, and he made me sit up. He pushed my head down between my knees and rubbed my back and told me to breathe and calm down. He stroked my hair and pressed up close to me in a nice sort of way, and I felt my lungs begin to fill.

After some full breaths, I fell back against the mattress with my head on Frank's pillow and shut my eyes. God, I were tired! There were a soreness in my chest, and my tears slipped hotly over my face. Frank lay beside me.

'Luella,' he whispered, and his finger wiped some wet off my cheek. 'I wouldn't have known you.'

'My ma's dead because of what you and that whore did.'

He sighed, and I heard him rub his face, the whiskers scratching against his palm. 'You're not a widow, are you?'

'She killed herself. She were in an asylum. Been in there three years.'

He cursed, but he said it so softly that it didn't sound like it were a bad word.

'You both made sure no one would believe a word what came out of her mouth after Pa. Not even her own ma. But she knew. She knew Pa were innocent. Want to know what she did to herself?'

He didn't say nothing; he most likely didn't want to know, but I were going to tell him anyway.

Three years I hadn't spoke of that day; Grandma wouldn't allow talk of it. It were like one of them awful family secrets except the whole of Bridgefield knew; it were this underlying thing what no one ever spoke about, but they showed their knowledge in the way they looked at you sideways or the way they chose their words too carefully.

'She jumped into the river. The children saw her do it and thought she were going for a swim, only she never came up for air. Some man dived in for her, nearly drowned himself. She were filthy when he brought her up to Grandma's. She were crying, saying she just wanted to be with Pa. It were like I weren't even in the room.'

Another tear swelled and spilled over. Frank brushed it away again.

'You did that to her,' I said. 'Pa were her whole life. There were no reason for her to keep living if he weren't beside her.'

'You think I killed Nicholas Campbell?'

'I know you did.' I jerked my head away from him. 'I saw you that night running away. You was in it together, you and that Bonnie woman. I know what you did.'

'It wasn't me, Luella.'

'And it weren't my pa, neither!'

'I know.'

I were stunned for a moment; no one had ever agreed with me about it before – except for Ma, of course.

'What do you mean?'

'Your father didn't kill that man.'

'Who, then?'

'Bonnie.'

'But …' I thought of the murder, of all that blood. A gruesome end. A murder done by a man, so everyone said. Women don't kill like that; they use poisons or something more ladylike.

I thought of Bonnie, only a girl back then, not much older than me now. I thought of how prim and proper she were in her pretty dresses and fancy hats and couldn't imagine it. Maybe she'd planned it and had Frank do it for her, but I couldn't believe that she did it all – that he were innocent.

'I don't believe you.'

'That's what happened.'

'Why did you run then?'

'She told me to go. I'd heard her shouting and I'd gone inside and found him dead. I wasn't going to stick around after that, even though she said she'd been defending herself.'

'Why? Didn't you believe her?'

'It's hard to believe anything that Bonnie says.'

'I saw you two' – I rolled over so I could look at him properly – 'in the barn, kissing. You was lovers, wasn't you? You was in it together from the start.'

'It depends what you mean by lovers.'

'Don't joke with me! You was together. You lied to Mrs Campbell about yourselves.' He was nodding as if he didn't care. 'You both killed Nicholas, and you both had my pa done for it!'

'No. Bonnie killed him. It was Bonnie, Luella, not me. I just left before anyone could point the finger my way; you'd have done the same.'

'I would not have let an innocent man hang!'

He chuckled at this and I hit him – that stopped him laughing. He faced me square on, all serious and frightening again. 'You were going to kill me tonight if you'd got the chance. What would that make you, Luella? You'd be worse than me.'

'I would have put things straight. It would've been justice!'

'You'd have killed the wrong person.' He cupped my face with his hand and came a little closer. The fog in his eyes from before had lifted, and his breath seemed a little sweeter. 'You want justice? You need to find Bonnie.'

CHAPTER 9

I'd never had a pain in my head like it when I woke up. It were like someone were slicing into my brain every time I moved. My body, too, were stiff. My hands was sore, as if I'd sanded my skin off. And when I slowly rolled to one side, there were a snag in my private parts.

I didn't know where I were for a while. I didn't understand the shape of things: the great big chest in the room, the colour of the quarry tiles, the smell of someone strange.

Sitting up, the pain got worse everywhere. I had to put my hand to my eyes because it felt as if they might burst out their sockets. My tummy were tight, and I looked for the piss pot and had to make a dash for it. My God, it didn't half burn as it came out! It were as if I'd been fair on torn apart.

And then it came back to me.

Frank. I'd been so tired, so sad. And he weren't my enemy after all. I were in shock. And his kisses had started to feel nice on my lips. He were gentler than what he had been before when he thought me just some widowed whore, and though I'd been scared, I didn't stop him.

He weren't in the room now. I peeked through the

curtain. Birds fluttered not far off the glass, some of them coming to the window frame to peck off a spider. Through the bushes what offered some privacy, I could see a patch of road and a donkey cart passing by. I could hear a bit of hammering nearby too and flinched each time the metal struck.

All the world were awake.

I thought of Grandma. I'd never been away before. Each morning had always started the same. I'd have been bent over the board by now, scrubbing away, cutting off slices of soap and rubbing them into someone else's clothes. And here I were, just lingering in nothing but my shift, as if I had nothing to be getting on with.

I dressed myself quick and crept into the rest of the house. It were more pleasant with the sunshine coming in through the back windows, and the kitchen didn't seem quite as poky as it had done the night before. The fire were going, the kettle had boiled once already this morning by the feel of it, and I set to making two cups of tea.

It were odd, wandering round a stranger's kitchen, seeing bits of their lives in what they had and what they didn't. Frank had a little food here and there, some of it green with mould. He must have plenty of money if he could let food grow shrivelled. There was a few iron pots and pans and one cracked bowl. The teacups was fair on dainty for a man like him; they wouldn't have looked out of place in a lady's parlour during afternoon tea, though the patterns on them had started to fade, and there was little sharp chips round the rims. But the main thing that Frank's cottage didn't have were the female touch.

Grandma, for all her sins, had paper decorations what she'd carefully cut out of newspapers and strung across the shelves. The Queen were forever staring at me in Grandma's cottage from above the fireplace, all toity and judging. We had rag rugs to stop the chill of the earth floor. Most of the time there was sheaths of herbs hanging off the beams and drying and making the air smell nice, and always we had an old jug sprouting flowers from the garden what we'd picked ourselves.

Frank had none of that. Everything seemed hard. If it had no purpose, you wouldn't find it. And there were a layer of dust over everything what made you feel as if you needed a good wash.

I didn't think about washing (I didn't think about the dirt what were on me and inside me because if I did, I think I might've screamed) as I poured the tea and went in search of him. I kept close to the house, not wanting to be seen by nosy folk, and found that the hammering were coming from the smithy. I had the sudden fear that I'd walk into it and find a host of men staring back at me, so I peered round the opening, ready to run at any minute, but it were only Frank inside. He were almost black already, and his sleeves was rolled up to his elbows showing the muscles in his forearms, and I had a thought that them arms, them hands, had been all over me last night. My face felt as hot as the white metal he were striking. I watched him for a good few minutes with all these funny feelings tumbling about inside me before he put his hammer down, wiped his brow, and looked up and saw me.

'Morning.' He did a proper big smile what showed all his teeth and made the lines round his eyes get even longer.

I stepped inside, making sure I didn't knock anything over or catch my dress on something, and gave him his tea. Then there were silence between us, because we was strangers to each other, after all. I watched my tea and the ripples when I blew on it.

'Nice day,' Frank said, going to the opening of the smithy and leaning on the wooden frame to look outside.

'Grandma'll be wondering where I am.'

'Do you care?'

'Not really.' She'd give me a thrashing when I got back if she could catch me. And then I suddenly realised something. 'I can't go back. I mean, I'll get my things, but I can't stay there.' The thought of my life stretching out the same as it had done these last eight years made me sick.

'What will you do?' He glanced over his shoulder at me, and I could have sworn he looked almost hopeful.

I just shrugged. It were too early to go talking about what were really on my mind.

'You can stay here.' He faced the view again, and when I didn't reply he said, 'At least until you know what your plans are.'

'Thank you.'

I went over to him and I were shaking – though I'd never admit to it – as I kissed him on the cheek. I think he blushed, but it were hard to be sure, what with all the grime on his face.

'I need to think,' I said, and ducked under his arm to return to the house.

I PASSED most of the day just sitting at the kitchen table and watching the birds play outside. It seemed a nice place, Ulstone, quiet but for the coaches what came through every so often and the shouting of the seagulls. It were a good place to do some thinking, and as I were thinking, I cleaned off Ma's locket with some vinegar and salt until the rust came off and the pewter had a bit of a shine to it.

Frank came in, and I made him tea and cut us bread and cheese for dinner, like we was some kind of married couple, until the sun had fallen out the sky and he came in for the last time. He said he went to the pub for his supper most nights but tonight he would stay in with me, and again we ate bread and what were left of a bit of hard cheese, and Frank opened a new bottle of whiskey because he'd finished the other one last night.

He watched me as we ate. If ever I caught him looking, he didn't try to hide what he were doing; he just smiled.

'So, you was with that Bonnie?' I said as I were chewing my last bit of crust. He went a bit shifty at the mention of her name.

'Still am.'

I didn't think I'd heard him right. The bread turned stale in my mouth, and though I tried, I just couldn't get it down, so I spat it on to my plate.

'Not properly. I don't love her, Luella. It's been a long time since I've loved her.'

'Then what do you mean, you're still with her?'

'We have an … arrangement.'

I really did think I might have spewed all over the table. I had to have a little walk round the kitchen to stop myself from going for him again.

'Calm down, love, please.' He went to touch me as if it were just a tiff we was having: a married couple's tiff. I flinched away from him, and taking the kettle what had been heating over the fire, I thrust it at him like it were a weapon. God knows what I'd've done with it, but I must have looked threatening enough because he backed off.

'All right, all right.' He brushed his hand over his face. 'Let me show you.'

WELL, you'd never've believed it if you hadn't seen it – the amount of silver and gold and jewels and bits of porcelain what was in that trunk in the bedroom! Bursting with it, it were. Getting on for three feet deep of the stuff. I just stared at it, my mouth hanging open as Frank presented it to me.

'For my silence,' he said.

'I don't understand.'

'It's all from Bonnie.'

'Where does she get it from?'

'Old women who thinks she's their friend.'

As if I hadn't been feeling sick enough! 'Mrs Campbell?'

He nodded, and I really did curse Bonnie then. The language what flew off my tongue! My dear Mrs Campbell, bled dry by a leech like Bonnie.

'You took this, Frank. You're just as bad.'

He didn't have the cheek to deny it, and I were at least grateful for that. 'I know what I am, Luella. I was a boy who never had anything, and I won't say no to things that I never stole in the first place if they can make my life easier. And it's not all for me anyway. She sends it to me thinking we'll live on it one day, that we'll go abroad and live like kings on her thieving.'

'And you don't think the same?'

'Not anymore.' He were rubbing his chin again, and I had an awful notion that he were on the edge of saying something what would change everything. I thought about running, but I were too late. 'I don't love her, Luella. I haven't loved her for years.'

'Does she love you?'

'Bonnie doesn't love anything but money. She's a cold-hearted bitch.'

Well, I weren't going to argue. I'd just called her worse, and I didn't even know her then.

'I've been thinking today, while I've been working, and you've been in here, in my home.' His lips pulled up into a little smile. 'It's been so nice having a woman here with me. It was never like that with Bonnie. Anyway,' he said, and he shook his head as if he wished he hadn't mentioned her name again, 'what I wanted to say was, I was thinking, with you saying you never wanted to go back to your grandmother's ... what if you stayed with me?'

The thought of it repulsed me, but he were looking with big, sad eyes, so I just said, 'Here?'

'No, not here. She knows where we are here. We'll go abroad. We'll leave with all that' – he nodded at the trunk – 'and we'll be gone before she knows it.' He were getting all excited. He came before me, took my hands, and pulled on me, trying to make me see sense.

'I can't.' I walked away from him, away from that vile trunk, and sat at the table. The sky outside were starting to look like cloudy water as the daylight faded. I heard his shoes scuffing on the tiles as he dragged his feet into the kitchen.

'I think I ... What I mean is, I like you, Luella.'

He'd known me less than a full day! Grandma had told me men was half stupid, their main sense coming from their privates, but I were still shocked at how quickly he could think himself in love.

Now, I'd never been too smart myself, never claimed to be. Pa used to get all huffy when he tried to teach me to read and write because I were always getting things mixed up. He'd do a tight smile and shut the book and say it were time for a biscuit, but I knew he just couldn't bear to be beside me another moment. And, as I said, I'd not had any experience with boys or men. But I had a thought while I were sitting there, with my private parts still sore and reminding me that now I really were a woman and that my ma were dead and that I were all alone and only had myself to rely on, that it would do me no harm to keep Frank close, for a while at least.

'Where might we go?' I said.

My God, if he were a dog I think he'd've peed himself, he were that thrilled.

'America. We can sail from Bristol and be in New York before autumn.'

'What would we do?'

'We wouldn't do anything! We'd have servants to do it all. You'd have your own maid to wait on you, and I'd have a valet, and we'd have footmen going about in the finest outfits you could imagine.'

I made myself smile back at him though he were talking nonsense. 'I'd like that.'

He let out a real long breath like he'd been holding it in for years. 'We can go now – tomorrow! There's nothing here for me. We'll go at night so no one sees us. I know a man with a cart who can take the trunk and us for a payment, and we can be at the docks … we can be on the boat before the week is out!'

'There's something I must do before we go, Frank.'

He swallowed, and I could see he were trying not to lose his spirit. 'All right.'

I gripped his hands, made my eyes nice and wide. 'Will you help me?'

'Of course, I will. What is it?'

'I must kill Bonnie.'

I WORRIED he'd turn on me, say that he'd been having me on and that he really did love Bonnie still, but he showed no qualms at my suggestions. He even added some of his own.

I were to claim I were looking for him and go on and on about killing him, and he knew that Bonnie couldn't let me find him – and all her thieving – all by myself. Because, you see (he said this quite mutteringly), he thought she might love him after all and wouldn't want to see harm done to him.

So I were to find her and act as if I knew all about her to scare her. I were to say I were looking for a man but couldn't remember his name – that would be my reasoning for tracking her down. Then I were to say my intentions of killing him.

Frank would do his part, he assured me, and together we'd lure her to the cottage.

Now, tell the truth, I were not too sure of all this. I'd only just been sneering at Frank for claiming he loved me after only knowing me some hours, and there I were trusting him when I knew him to be a thief and a murderer's accomplice! But, see, I didn't have much other choice. The rage that were in me whenever I thought of Bonnie ... I could have gone up in flames with it. I were blinded by it, in all honesty.

The light had started to bleed into the sky again when Frank kissed me and promised me the world. He took me to bed and had his way with me one last time. I didn't flinch at the pain; I were too impatient to feel it. The soles of my feet was itching; I wanted to be on my way to Bonnie. She couldn't be dead quick enough.

I watched Frank as he slept; I couldn't rest for them final few hours. His mouth were open, and he were drooling as he snored beside me. He were a bit like Pa in looks, I realised as I studied him, what with his thick, dark hair and the general handsomeness of him, though Pa must have been smaller because he were only a bookkeeper, and never once did I see him use tradesmen's tools or do any heavy lifting.

With this in my head, I couldn't look at Frank no longer without feeling ill, so I got up and dressed. I woke him and wished him farewell and had to keep still as he kissed me with his morning breath and said how he wished I'd stay a little longer. I said I wished the same, but time were running away from us if we was to be in America by September. Then I patted his cheek and scarpered.

I walked a fair few miles before a coach came by, and then I sat as patiently as I could until the stop for Bridgefield, at which point I jumped off and hurried through the town. I didn't take no notice of nobody, and before I knew it, I were back at Grandma's cottage, and it were like I'd never been gone. I could have walked in and rolled up my sleeves and got on with the day's work if Grandma hadn't come flying out through the door like a goose, honking at me.

I ducked under her blows. She were still coming for me as I were tearing off my dress, and for a while I let her hit me, but then I'd had enough. I were down to my shimmy when she went for my head again, and I caught her arm and held her still as she struggled. I held her tighter and tighter until her hand started to turn red, and then I stared at her straight in the face and saw what I'd never seen in her before: fear.

I let go. Both of us was breathing hard, but we didn't say nothing to each other. I pulled out Ma's old dress what I'd folded neatly in my bag at the asylum, and put it over me. Grandma gasped. I think she might have crossed herself had she been Catholic. I understood why when I saw my reflection in the rusted old looking glass. I were the spit of Ma.

I turned away before my tears came and stalked out the bedroom. Near Grandma's chair next to the fire were the flask she kept for night times. She'd made a new batch of medicine from the poppies in the garden some weeks previous, and I took off the lid and saw that the flask were almost full.

'I'm taking this.' I put it into my bag. She went to protest, but I give her such a stare that she backed off.

On the windowsill, there was a few more pennies since last time, but I left them. I had no need of them after Frank had give me a couple of pound notes – more of Bonnie's fortune.

'You won't see me again,' I said, as I looked round what I'd known to be my home for the last eight years. I were sure not an inch of me would miss it.

'What nonsense you spouting, now?'

'Ain't nonsense. I ain't never coming back, Grandma.'

The look of fear went over her again, and for a moment I almost felt sorry for her, but then her face hardened into a sneer. 'And where is it Lady Muck thinks she's going?'

'None of your business. From now on you can think me as dead as your daughter, and I'll think the same of you.'

She flinched at that. Nothing so mean had come from my mouth before, at least, not about my own family, not outside of my own brain. I felt thrilled by it a bit and wanted to say something else what would sting her, because she'd stung me plenty times before now, but at the same time there were a burning in my cheeks what I knew to be shame, so I kept my mouth shut.

I marched away from Grandma and her cottage at the edge of the woods for the very last time that lovely summer afternoon. I didn't look back once.

CHAPTER 10

Stowmouth were quite a nice town, though it had the smell of old fish blowing in the wind and there were gull shit everywhere. But it were big enough that no one took much notice of a stranger, and there was rooms to rent easily.

I found a friendly looking grocer as I were strolling through the streets. He had a belly what made him look like he were expecting and cheeks what was flushed. It turned out he had a room of his own to rent, and he showed me upstairs, pushing on the mattress to show that it were soft, opening his arms wide to show just how spacious it were, beckoning me to the window so that I might see what a nice view it had over the town and of the church not too far off. I took it without asking the price, and he brought me up a pot of tea as I settled in. I told him I'd be staying only a few nights at most, and then I wrote to Frank to tell him my address.

That first night, after going to the post office just a few doors down the street to send the letter, I couldn't move from the chair by the window. I just stared at the church, for I knew that beyond it were Bonnie.

I imagined myself flying over the thatched roofs, over the tip of the spire, over the green, and crashing through one of her windows. I kept playing the flight over and over in my mind so that at one point it truly did feel as if there were air billowing underneath me. When I opened my eyes again, the sky outside were black – how the time had passed! I made myself go to bed and lie down so that I'd be thinking straight for the morning.

I must have slept a bit because a bang downstairs startled me, and I realised it were the grocer opening up for the day. I went downstairs and outside, saying a quick hello and that I'd slept like a baby, and then I went to the sea.

It were one of them perfect summer mornings. The sky were pale, pale blue. The beach had lovely golden sand as if it had been toasted. Fishing boats bobbed gently out on the calm waters.

I sat there for a few hours just looking at it all. To the left of me and out of the boundaries of the town, a red-faced cliff rose up out of the sea. The town were held in its shadow until the sun got higher up, and then the new buildings behind me twinkled and sparkled like shells polished by the waves.

The fishing boats came back in for the day, and when my backside had lost all its feeling, I went to a man selling cones of cockles and ate them as I wandered about.

I were putting it off, see. I'd come all this way and got myself all worked up, and now I were dreading seeing Bonnie. I fair on had to drag my own feet towards that church, where I had to lean on the stonework for a while before I could carry on over the green.

It were mid-afternoon by this point, and lots of ladies was out taking their afternoon strolls. They didn't like the looks of me one bit, so I kept to the sides and tried to hide myself in the shade of the trees until I had a good view of Bonnie's home.

It weren't a bit like Mrs Campbell's house. That one had been ramshackle and made of red brick, with bits of new rooms added on here and there over the years. Chimneys had stuck up all over the place, and barns and outbuildings had been dotted about haphazardly. It had dirt tracks all around it, and the grounds had been taken over by animals and the wild.

This house here were all very neat, like a box what'd been stretched skywards. It were painted bright white, and it hurt your eyes to look at it when the sun were full on it. It had a sharp set of black iron railings hemming it in, and the plants inside them railings was trimmed nice and smart. It didn't look like the sort of place what kept animals.

I sat on one of the benches under a tree and waited for a sign of life. Not a single one came for ages. The church bell chimed half past two, then three, then half past. The wind picked up with each tolling of them bells, and the sound of the leaves rustling around me drowned out everything else. So bored I was, I took to watching the sky. Clouds had started to build, and they was scudding along in the wind so fast that they looked like sailing ships. It were as I were watching one white cloud go whipping along that something caught my eye: movement in one of the windows.

The angles made it so that I couldn't get a good view from my bench. I had to walk to the middle of the green until I could see inside properly, and then I really were rooted to the spot.

I don't know what I'd been expecting. A monster? But Bonnie had never looked like a monster. She were in a light grey gown covered with a little white apron, and she were in the window on the top floor. She held a dusting cloth in one hand and one of her mistress's trinkets in the other. She hadn't changed much in eight years, maybe a little plumper, maybe slightly softened with age. But her hair were still as dark as one of Mrs Campbell's mahogany tables. Her skin were still the colour of coffee laced with cream. I would never have called her pretty. My ma were pretty, the prettiest girl in Bridgefield; Bonnie were more ... striking. She weren't the kind of woman you'd see every day. She were unusual in her beauty.

I were just noting how she'd changed or stayed the same and feeling all them funny feelings brewing up in me again, when blow me down but she didn't just slip that little trinket what she'd been polishing into her apron pocket! She did it so casual and then picked up another trinket off the windowsill, dusted it, and put it back in its place as if she didn't have something stolen in her pocket at all. She hadn't changed one bit!

Suddenly, she stopped what she were doing and looked out the window and straight at me. I couldn't move; I were a little girl again what had been caught with her fingers in the jam. A frown came on her face, she cocked her head to one side, and I thought she were going to remember me and do something dramatic, like wave at me or run outside to meet me, but then she stopped frowning and put her head back on straight, and her face went hard.

We stood looking at each other for a fair few moments. My stomach were bubbling – all them cockles rolling around. Part of me wanted to run for her and grab her by them dark locks and drag her out kicking and screaming. Part of me wanted to turn tail and flee. She were all too real. All of this were too real. I thought if I looked at her another moment I would be sick.

Then there were a bang from somewhere in the house what made my heart come into my mouth. I turned and I ran. When I were back in the safety of my rented room looking across at the church spire, God how I cursed myself for my own cowardice!

THE NEXT DAY I vowed I would not be so weak. After some hours on the beach, I marched all the way to Bonnie's house before my feet had chance to stop.

I waited in the shade of a tree by the house railings, for it were a blasted hot day with no breeze to speak of. I scanned the windows, and then below me (there were a short flight of steps what led down to a narrow yard and a basement area), in what I assumed must have been the scullery, I saw movement. I half wondered whether to make a dash for it because I didn't think Bonnie would lower herself so much as to be working in the kitchens, but then a door opened, and she were walking towards me before I knew it.

She came right up to me, bold as anything, and folded her arms across her chest, looking most displeased.

'Bonnie Hearn?' My voice were queer to my own ears, as if I'd been strangled. I coughed to try and make it strong again, but I were losing my nerve. I needed something; I needed Ma. I held the chain and thought of her and what this woman, who were standing in front of me so brazenly, had done to her, and my hands stopped trembling.

She asked who I were, but I weren't ready to tell her just yet. It were enough to have come this far, and I needed to stay in control, so I told her she were to meet me in the tea room I'd found earlier that day.

I'd had an idea to get her on her own because it were dangerous for me to be seen with her by someone she knew. I thought a tea room in the town would be well enough; as I said, there was so many folks on holiday, so many strangers coming in and out the place, no one would take much notice of us in a tea room.

Bonnie started shaking her head, saying it weren't possible. I were losing patience with her. If she'd kept on being so ignorant and up herself, I'd have surely throttled her, so I took a breath and said over her, 'I know Miss Grey likes to sleep then, and I know how you fills your time when she does so.'

The threat seemed to work; it shut her up anyway. She smirked at me as if I were the most amusing thing she'd seen all day, and by God, it took some strength for me not to smack that smirk right off her face! I nodded and turned away before I did anything I'd regret.

The following afternoon, I stood by my window watching the town below, waiting for the three church bells. I had to grip the back of the chair to stop me fidgeting. I were feeling so sick, as if I were all wrung up inside like one of Grandma's wet sheets when we squeezed the water out of it.

The bells chimed. Would she be at the tea room? She didn't strike me as the sort what would be late for an appointment. Maybe she'd be sitting at a table right now, and here I were, biding my time.

All night and all morning I'd been mulling over the conversation I'd have with her. I'd played out imaginary scenarios: she'd suss me out straight away and call a policeman on me; she'd turn vicious and scald me with the teapot; she'd break down crying and admit to everything and hand herself over to justice. I'd thought of everything, and still I could not decide whether to take the handkerchief with me or not.

I went for my bag and got it out and stared at it as if it

would answer for itself. Curse it, I thought, and shoved it up my sleeve and made for the door, but then I hesitated. I pulled the handkerchief back out. Maybe it would scare her off, after all. So I put it away, and by the time I'd done all this, the church bells was ringing again, and fifteen minutes had passed!

I were sweating when I reached the tea room, almost half an hour late. I thought she'd be gone, that I'd missed my opportunity. All that time thinking things through, worrying about stuff, and I'd never get to actually talk to her!

I couldn't see for a moment when I stepped into that tea room. It were so dark in there compared to the sunshine. It smelt kind of off, and really, I had no clue why the women what was in there looked at me like they did (like I were something what they'd found on their shoe) because it weren't the kind of place you could boast about.

Once my eyes had got used to the gloom, I searched for Bonnie. My heart were just about sinking when I discovered her tucked up in one corner, her fancy frock blending in with the patterned wallpaper and fringed lamps.

I sat quickly; I didn't want the other customers to remember my face too much. My head were itching with all the heat from under my bonnet and my skin were prickling – that kind of prickle that could've been from the sun or could've been just my own nerves.

The table were already cluttered with tea things, all very distracting. And then Bonnie asked for more tea, and the waitress brought it over, and the space on the table shrank even more, and, oh God, but I found it all such a nuisance! Why had I chosen to meet her in a tea room? It were all too closely packed in, and the walls looked as if they had hands on the other sides of them squeezing them together. It were noisy with the women whispering amongst themselves and Bonnie pouring the tea and the tap of the spoon against the china as she stirred the liquid round and round …

I grabbed the cup and drank. It were hot, but not scalding. I hadn't had sugar with my tea for years, and the taste were comforting. Bonnie said something, but I couldn't hear her; I were years away, drinking tea with my ma in the parlour and laughing at something I couldn't now remember. And by the time I'd come to the end of my drink, the tea room didn't seem quite so small or loud, and the prickling of my skin had stopped, and I could breathe properly again.

Bonnie were waiting for me to say something. She were looking at me expectantly.

'You don't remember me,' I said.

She shook her head. How were it that she didn't remember someone whose life she had destroyed?

'You knew my father. Samuel Blyth.'

Well, you should have seen her face fall when I told her his name! That were confirmation enough in that one look, better than any confession she could've give from her own lips. I felt like standing up right there and saying *Ha! I have you now!* But I didn't say nothing, I just watched her as her memories took her back all them years until she looked at me again. My name were on the tip of her tongue, I could tell.

'Luella,' I said, to put her out her misery.

'What do you want, Luella?'

'A name.'

She laughed, but it were one of them stiff laughs what didn't think something were funny at all. That's when I played the whole game of trying to get Frank's name out of her. She weren't giving it up easy, and he'd been right to say she still thought something of him; why else would she try to cover up her knowledge of him? But I got it out of her in the end, and I fair on put the wits up her when I told her I knew about all the women she'd worked for. When I said I planned on killing Frank, well, she went whiter than me!

I moved quick out the tea room. To be truthful, I were so pleased with myself that I couldn't stop grinning – I got some stares from the folks I passed on the street, I tell you! I couldn't believe it'd been so easy. Our plan were actually working. And if Frank were right, it wouldn't be long before she were trying to catch me up and stop me from doing what I were planning on.

I slowed my step a bit because I didn't want her to lose me. Sneaking a glance over my shoulder, I saw her come out the tea room and stagger with the brightness of the day. I rounded the corner just as her face turned my way. I used the shop windows as looking glasses and, sure enough, there she were in the reflections, running after me.

I got to the grocer's and waved hello at him as I waited, looking at his vegetable display.

'Luella!'

Could I stop the smile on my face? No, I could not.

I WAITED in the next day and the day after. It rained, and I had no intention of getting Ma's dress wet seeing as it were the only one I had with me. Nor did I know when Bonnie would be calling in to see me, and I didn't want to miss her. So I sat by the window looking out over Stowmouth and breathing in the air what the rain had washed fresh, daydreaming of killing her.

I'd taken Grandma's flask, and half a cup of its contents would have Bonnie sleeping before she knew it. That would give me time to string her up without her struggling. I'd wait until the medicine had wore off and she were just waking up, and then I'd be able to see the horror on her face when she knew she were about to die. Frank must have some rope somewhere, I thought, and I wanted her to go the same way as Pa had gone. And if that proved too troublesome, maybe I'd stab her wrists like Ma had and watch her bleed out.

It were as I were thinking this that a beautiful flash of blue caught my eye. Bonnie were on her way.

I arranged myself by the door and heard her talking to the grocer in that toity way of hers and then her footsteps coming up the stairs. When she knocked, I counted to three before I answered.

She took a good look around as she stepped inside and crinkled her nose at everything. She thought I might've done a runner, she said, but I reminded her that she promised she'd help me.

I were taking it all very tongue-in-cheek for a while, I have to say. She were still a bit jumpy like she were the day before yesterday, but it were clear she'd been thinking and that she had a plan in mind. And I knew that her plan were to keep me on her side, to lead me up the garden path before trying to kill me, because I'd got a letter from Frank that morning telling me about it. Here she were, trying to put one over on me when I were the one playing her from the start!

But then she did something I weren't expecting. She pulled out a little gold ring on a chain round her neck and said she were married to Frank.

Well, he'd never mentioned that! I thought it were just another one of her lies for a second; the ring could've been something else she'd stolen from a mistress. But there were something about it … the way she held it real gentle, the way it were hidden behind her gown and next to her heart, the way she put it back inside her bodice and seemed to relax once it were on her skin. It were how I were with Ma's locket, like she had a real love for it.

I cursed myself for it after, but at the time, I couldn't help but feel sad for her. She were in love with him, and he were plotting to do her over.

She tried pleading with me again, for my own sake as well as Frank's. She were getting careless in her desperation; her mouth were running away from her. My pity started to wear. I pulled myself together, told myself to stick to the plan.

'Whatever he has done? You know what he's done?'

She admitted Frank were the murderer. I'd never seen someone lie so easy. And about the man they was supposed to be in love with too. She were pinning it on him to save herself. That set the rage up in me again, and I thought, curse you, Bonnie Hearn; I'll have you strung up on a pole if it's the last thing I do!

I went a bit crazy on her. I locked her in and wouldn't give over the key until she said where he were. She made out that Frank were such a terrible, violent man, what'd beaten her up before, but however much she tried to scare me off, I were having none of it.

'I will kill him!' I screamed the words, and as I said them I weren't thinking of Frank, I were thinking of her and just how much I wanted to hurt her. I knew I couldn't though, not there. My pulse were throbbing so fast, and I'd got myself in such a state that the only thing I could do were cry.

She tried comforting me and made me sit by her on the bed and had me weep against her. She stroked my back and cooed to me as if she actually cared about me, but all it did were make me think of my ma and how it should've been her there to comfort me and hold me. Bonnie's lies had made that impossible.

'How can you stand it?' I whispered. Part of me really did want to know how she could've lived all these years without dying of a guilty conscience. 'How can you bear to know what you know and live with it?'

She mistook my meaning, of course, and thought I were

talking about Frank being a murderer. I realised then that I'd get nowhere feeling sorry for myself and wishing things was different. Things was as they was. Only the future were mine to change.

'You could be free of him,' I said, and she kept still and listened. 'Do you love him?'

'Not anymore.' It sounded like a lie, but how could I be sure?

'Then let us kill him.'

Again, she made a show of saying it were impossible. I let her talk herself round in circles until she took control and said the plan what she'd had in her mind the whole time.

'Arsenic. Kill Frank with arsenic.'

'How?'

'Fly papers. I shall lead you to Frank. I shall ready the poison. I shall keep him oblivious to our plan. And then you may pour him some tea and watch him drink it and watch him die.'

It were perfect.

The arsenic would be meant for me, of course. That's how she'd chosen to kill me. She were already a murderer anyway, one more on her conscience would mean nothing. And there she were, acting all nice and like a good little woman, and not a flicker of guilt passed over her face. By God, it made me laugh!

'You really are something, Bonnie.'

CHAPTER 11

I couldn't sleep that night. I packed and re-packed my bag in the glow of the candlelight, and in the small hours, I set that candle on the table and snuck out of the room. I had to leave by the back door, and I came out in an alleyway what smelt of piss because it were so close to the privies.

In Stowmouth, most of the windows was dark and the streets quiet, but every now and then as I went by a narrow passage I heard noises what was unusual to me. I tried to tell myself it were foxes because foxes was always causing mischief, but I weren't really that stupid. Men and whores lurked in the shadows. I walked quicker, keeping my gaze on the looming black mass of the church so I wouldn't see anything what didn't want to be seen.

The moon and stars lit my way, and I sat where I had the other day on that bench and watched the house.

It were a really lovely night. A barn owl swooped not far off, real foxes barked, mice rustled somewhere nearby. Their squeaks made me think of the time when one of Mrs Campbell's cats had caught a mouse. It were a bloody sight. I'd found it on the stone step by the back door. All its fur were matted with red gloop, and then it moved.

I scooped it up and took it into the kitchen. Mrs Campbell didn't scream or shout at me, she just took the mouse in her soft hands and held it close. The creature were struggling for breath as we sat beside the range. I cuddled up to Mrs Campbell's arm, and together we watched the mouse take its very last breath, and both of us shed a tear.

Nature can be cruel, she said, as she stroked its tiny head. The poor thing had emptied its bowels into her hands, and the yellow had seeped into the wrinkles of her palms, and I remembered thinking she'd been stained with death.

The memory made me cry. Slow tears trickled down my cheeks. She'd been such a kind woman. I felt my heart break again when I thought of how she'd spent her last days with the agony of grief.

But, mercifully, I couldn't dwell too long on that pain. The sky were lightening, and as it did, I heard the gentle click of a door being closed very carefully. Bonnie, with her posh leather case, crept up from the yard and tiptoed away from the house. I crouched behind the bench so I could see what she did.

She turned back to the house when she were on the green less than ten feet away from me. I could hear her breath blow in and out over her lips as she stood there real still, while I tried not to breathe at all. Her eyes flicked over the house, then rested on the top window. Her whole body quivered. Then, as if someone had called her name, she turned towards Stowmouth and strode over the green without looking back. I kept in the shadows as I followed her.

The town were waking up now. Windows glowed with candlelight, and the sinful sounds I'd heard only hours previous had gone.

Bonnie shone as she walked through the streets in her

blue dress. She made her way to the grocer's and stopped on the corner of the street a little way off, looking up at my window. I dipped into the shadow of a doorway some way behind her.

She pulled something out of a secret pocket in the lining of her skirts, something white and about the size of her palm, and then slid it into the post box.

So, a letter. To Frank, no doubt, confirming we was on our way.

She jumped out her skin when I said good morning to her, and she looked at the grocer's window where my candle-light shone in the gloom. Her face flushed. Caught red-handed!

I weren't about to gloat though. I didn't want her to know I'd seen what she were up to, so I took her hand and dragged her out of Stowmouth because there were no point waiting around. The day needed to start. The journey needed to begin. The plan needed to be put into action.

I were getting all giddy with the excitement of it as Stowmouth fell away behind us. I were pulling her along, using the river as a guide as I had done when I'd walked into town five days ago. I'd forgotten that I shouldn't have known where we was heading, and for a moment I thought I'd given the whole game away, but somehow I managed to convince her otherwise. She were too concerned with the state of her shoes to think too much about my error.

I bit my cheeks to stop me saying another word. I were getting too carried away. If I didn't get myself under control, I'd ruin everything. So I let Bonnie lead us out the valley and to the road and kept a pace or two behind her as we set off for Frank's cottage.

I SHAN'T REPEAT EVERYTHING; you know most of it already. I

shall tell only the important parts again. The other times, I were just holding my tongue and doing my utmost not to kill her.

That were until the coach trip and that awful man, Paul Meadows. God, he were a terrible sight, and he stank to high heaven. We thought him nothing more than a fool in that coach, and can you believe it, but we actually laughed together as we tormented him. I think both of us was taking out our frustrations on him because we couldn't take it out on each other.

But then Bonnie had to let him eat supper with us. I never understood that about her: her politeness, her need to please. She were forever smiling at people (apart from me, of course, though she had at the start when she didn't know she hated me). She made conversation with Paul as he got more and more drunk, and she didn't once say he'd had enough wine. I would've left them to it, but she'd set me up as a blasted maid for her, and even I knew it would look odd for a maid to leave her mistress alone with a strange man. And really, it weren't a bad cover for me, to be her maid. No one takes no notice of a maid. No one looked twice at me when they heard of my station. Bonnie got all the attention. And that were just fine with me. I didn't want my face printed and stuck up on sheets all over Somerset if ever they found her body.

But then that Paul Meadows turned nasty. I could see he would; his eyes was too close together. He were a bad drunk, one what liked to tease and thought himself hilarious at it too.

'What a pretty little thing you are, Lucy. How old are you, Lucy?' he said as we sat outside.

I focused on the silkiness of the willow branches. As if the stench of his breath hadn't been bad enough, he dared to touch my cheek. I were always cautious of anyone what went to touch me. Too often it had ended in a strike. Too often boys had reached for me only to pinch me and laugh. Paul Meadows were no different than them boys. I fair on whacked his hand away and growled at him.

I were all ready to set at him again when Bonnie got up and said she were tired. In truth, it were her way of trying to control the situation. She didn't want to cause a fuss, see; ladies didn't cause fusses. So up she stood, still smiling, though I could see there were something in her face, a stiffness what showed her unease. And that's when Paul went for her legs.

Well, I'd never known anything like it. For a strange man to go under the skirts of a lady! I think both me and Bonnie was stunned for a moment and unable to say anything but stare at him as he carried on pining and whining at her feet and pawing at her. It all kind of slowed down as I watched the two of them. I'd never seen Bonnie's face like that before, even when I'd talked of murder. She went very still and turned very pale, and she had such a look of terror about her that it made me feel scared too.

Paul clung on to her, his hands getting higher and higher. Her skirts was stretched, and the material were close on ripping. He pulled on her legs and she were juddering, and it suddenly reminded me so much of Pa's hanging that I couldn't move. I saw the hangman tugging on my pa's bound legs as he jerked like a puppet on a string.

And then a scream. My ma. Her face burnt red with rage and grief, streaked with tears as she bent over and yelled at the earth.

My own fists was balled tight; my legs couldn't hold me back. I pummelled Paul Meadows' body like I wished I'd been able to pummel that hangman eight years ago. I slashed at him and thumped him and didn't care for the ache and the swell of my own hands. I wanted to hear his bones break beneath me. I wanted him to fall at my feet so I could kick him and spit at him – anything to get him off my pa and stop my ma from shouting.

It were all a mess as someone came about me and held my arms by my sides. My feet was still kicking at the man curled up in a ball, and I managed to get one last blow to the side of his head with my boot before I were bundled away.

My anger went almost as quick as it had come. I saw the scene – Bonnie shaking and staring at Paul, the landlady fussing over her and stroking her like she were a spooked mare, the men from the pub muttering amongst themselves and frowning at me.

I were breathless. My pulse beat against my stays. My knuckles was all red, and I winced as I flexed my hand.

The landlady led Bonnie inside and I followed. The inn were empty; all the men was out there. The landlady took Bonnie up and told me to get a bottle of wine, and as I went behind the counter, I heard the men shouting at Paul Meadows and the sharp smack of a man's hand against another man's face.

I took the liberty of pouring myself a measure of rum and downing it in one while I were all alone. The strength of it brought me back to my senses.

'She's waiting for you,' the landlady said as she came downstairs. She weren't as nice to me as she were to Bonnie and looked me up and down like I weren't natural. I were too tired to care what she thought of me. I shoved past her with the bottle of wine in my hand.

Bonnie were sat on the bed, her eyes wide and wet. She were scared and needed comforting, and though it were the last thing I wanted to do, I couldn't just ignore her.

'Did he get to you? Properly?' I asked, because Bonnie had thanked me, and I were feeling a bit guilty; I'd only beaten him off because he'd reminded me of the hangman, after all.

She said she were fine, though it were obvious she weren't. It were like she couldn't move, and to save time and having to talk, I went to help her out of her dress. I think she thought I were going to strangle her or something because she went still, and I knew by then that when she went real still it meant she were frightened, but she started to relax by the time all her hair were out of its pins and her dress were off.

And then she were just stood there in her shimmy. I took the chance to look at her properly. The shape of her. The smoothness of her skin. The length and gloss of her hair. The foreign look of her face what made her seem exotic. What had she got, that's what I wanted to know? What had made her so special? What did she have what had made my pa blind to the rest of us?

I couldn't find the answer. As I said, I were too tired. I stopped looking at her for fear I'd say what I were thinking out loud and went to get her nightgown out of her case. There were a whole bundle of stolen trinkets wrapped in her dresses, and I wouldn't have given a single penny for any of them.

'It was my mother's husband,' she went on to explain, not that I'd been wanting any explanation. It did surprise me though; she were too calm and toity to have been fiddled with like that as a child – so it seemed to me anyway. I didn't think folk like her had that sort of thing happen to them.

'Didn't your ma stop him?'

'Mother didn't see what she didn't want to.'

My ma had been the same, though the circumstances couldn't have been more different.

I were just about to get into that horrible little pallet bed when Bonnie said I could come in with her. Well, I weren't so boiling with rage and disgust that I were going to refuse a good soft mattress for the night, even if it meant lying next to the likes of her. I kept myself at arm's length. My backside were half out the covers, but at least I were comfortable.

'How did you meet Frank?' I couldn't help it; I'd always been nosy. The room were so quiet it were like it were only me and her in the whole world. I didn't think it would matter to learn a bit about her.

She said about Frank being her stepfather's apprentice and what-not, and I were getting real drowsy with tiredness, but my ears pricked up when she said, 'Frank and I … we saved each other, you see. We got each other out of there.'

'You loved him.' You could hear it in her voice whenever she spoke of him, couldn't miss it.

A tear fell from her eye before she swiped it away.

'So much that it hurt.'

And that were the truth of it all, weren't it? That's why we was both here – because of love.

It seemed to me that there were only ever pain: my pa had hurt my ma; my ma had hurt me; Bonnie had hurt Pa and Ma and me all at the same time; and all of it because of love. The thought of it hit me and took the breath straight out my lungs.

'I suppose love always hurts.'

She tried to do a runner on me the next morning. I had a panic when I saw her side of the bed were empty, and I almost cried with relief when I saw her hobbling off down the road. She couldn't escape me that easy!

She did look a pathetic sight, with her dress hanging off her all floppy because she'd scarpered without her corset or her cage – how desperate she must've been to get away. She told me she were doing it for me and tried to give me a five-pound note so I could sail away to America without murder on my conscience.

For a moment, I thought about it. A part of me were getting a bit soft with her. A couple of times I'd found myself asking how her ankle were doing and thinking to myself whether or not she'd like something or other. I suppose it were just being so close with someone that you started to get used to them. Like I had been with Grandma; I'd hated her and at the same time I'd always made sure her tea weren't too hot to burn her lips, and I'd taken it on myself to cut the soap because I knew how stiff and swollen her knuckles got.

But I'd left Grandma with the last words that I wished her dead. And I'd known Bonnie less than a week, and most of that week I'd hated what I'd seen. And really, her plea for me to leave were only to save herself the hassle of having to deal with me, and I weren't about to make her life easy.

So on we went.

The air were so heavy that day it were like fingers pushing down your eyelids; it forced you to sleep. I woke up feeling sick as the coach rattled along. I were disorientated and sticky, but as I looked out the window, things seemed familiar. We weren't far off Bridgefield.

'Want to call in? Tell them what you're planning?' Bonnie were in a mood with me because I hadn't done what she'd wanted. She proper had a pout on her. 'How old are you?'

I said I were eighteen, that I'd been ten when Pa had swung. For the first time since meeting, she asked what had happened to me afterwards.

Progress, I thought; perhaps she were feeling some guilt. But she ruined it when I told her about Grandma's cottage, and she had the cheek to say it must be pretty in summer. Yes, pretty for a fool what don't have to live there! Pretty for someone what don't hate the very sight of it. I don't think she heard the sarcasm dripping from my voice as I told her about the flowers.

She'd riled me, and I were taking it out on her best I

could. I talked about tickling and if she thought men was only interested in that, and she said she didn't think so, but she said it in an odd way. The subject were making her go funny. She'd started to bite her lip, and her face were all shiny with sweat.

'Have you a handkerchief?'

The timing couldn't have been more perfect. Surely now, with her all edgy and jumpy, the handkerchief would do it, would make her confess. I gave it to her, and she neatened it out, and then she saw it – the stitching. It were like my pa's ghost had slapped her in the face. She didn't half go white. I thought she'd start crying or screaming or do something at least, but she just stared at it and stayed silent.

'He dropped it when he were being arrested,' I said, trying to prompt her, but she kept quiet. 'It were dirty from all the boots what trampled it, but we saved it.'

'We?' she said, and it were like someone had their hand round her throat and were squeezing hard.

'Ma and me.'

She didn't flinch when I mentioned my mother. She smoothed her fingers over the white cotton and the red letters like she were in a trance. 'It's clean now.'

Grandma had boiled and starched it until it sparkled. Ma had cried for days after because all Pa's scent had gone. Grandma told her to stop being so daft and to start looking for a new husband, one what'd marry the widow of a murderer and take on a petulant child what weren't his own.

'At least you have something to remember him by,' Bonnie said and tried to smile.

I snatched the handkerchief out of her quivering hands. Still, she would not confess.

Yes, it were the perfect thing to remember my pa by; it showed exactly the type of man he were. I shoved it inside my bag so I didn't have to look at it. I might have torn it to shreds otherwise.

Bonnie made us stop at another inn that day, saying she weren't up to getting to Frank's so soon. She were looking a bit green in the face. I didn't know whether this were to do with seeing Frank again or doing what she'd been planning on doing to me. Though I made a face and rolled my eyes, if truth be told, I were starting to get a bit worried too.

I went outside so I didn't have to watch her pick at her food. She'd changed over the days; she weren't quite so calm and calculating. I could see some of her truthfulness coming through in the way she did certain things like bite her lip or stare too long at me with soft eyes. Maybe her conscience really were catching up with her, and it made me think of my own conscience.

I sat there with the cat curling round me and let the sun bake me. Were it really worth it? Killing her wouldn't bring Ma or Pa back. It wouldn't make my childhood any better than it had been. Nothing could be changed. Nothing would stop the ache in my eyes and my guts whenever I remembered I'd never feel Ma's hand against my cheek again, nor hear her singing as she tended her favourite rose bush.

It were all too late.

Thinking like that were making my head hurt. I talked it over with the cat, but he didn't have much to say to me. He got a bit fed up of me and clawed me and drew a little drop of blood, and I took that to mean he were telling me I'd have blood on my hands. Who knew cats could be so smart?

I watched the wisps of cloud amble along in the sky as the sun went lower. I thought of the times before, when it had been just Ma and Pa and me, and how happy we'd been. For the first time in years, the memories didn't make me cry;

they made me smile. I sat there, remembering, until my legs started needling and my arse had turned numb and the cat meowed at me, and then I went to find Bonnie.

The bar were empty and the landlord nowhere to be seen (I were going to tell him the cat wanted feeding). I poured a saucer of milk for the cat and stayed with him while he drank it, and then I too were feeling parched from all the sun, so I got myself some water and crept upstairs.

Bonnie's door weren't locked. On the chest, there were a pen and ink pot what I hadn't noticed before, and as Bonnie were sleeping on top of the covers, I could make out the black splodges of ink on her right fingers. She lay with her head on the pillow and her hair spread out around her. As her chest rose and fell with each breath, her gold wedding band glinted in the light.

Her face weren't peaceful though; she kept frowning, and the corners of her eyes was a bit wet, and then she started saying stuff. A lot of it weren't clear, but I could make out some words like *no* and *stop that* and *please* and *go*. It weren't a nice sight, tell the truth, and I had a sudden urge to wake her and kiss her forehead and tell her she were only dreaming, but then the cat jumped on the pillow beside her, and the movement roused her a little. When she didn't wake, I nudged her arm.

'You was talking,' I said, because she looked alarmed to find me so close. She asked what she'd been saying, wondering, I imagined, whether she'd given anything of herself away.

'He's gone, the landlord. I can't find him nowhere.'

Her gaze darted straight to her blackened fingers, and I knew that she must have sent him with a note of some kind to Frank; we was less than five miles from Ulstone. But I didn't want the hassle of calling her out on it.

Instead, I couldn't take my eyes off that gold ring on her

chest. The gleam on it – how she must polish it! The simplicity of it – with most other things, she had a fancy for decoration. I wondered if she'd been holding on to it as she'd fallen asleep, as if it might have been a child's soft blanket.

'What's it like to be in love, Bonnie?'

'We talked about that yesterday.' She returned my glass of water, what she'd drunk herself, to the table.

'Love hurts, you said, and I can believe that. But there must be more. There must be joy. Why would anyone do it if there were no joy in it?'

It were a proper question – I weren't asking it to rile her; I truly wanted to know. I wanted to know what love were like between a man and a woman because I'd never known it and couldn't understand it. It seemed to cause such trouble and so many complications – sometimes it were even fatal – that I didn't know why anyone would want to love at all. Better to feel nothing than feel so much pain.

'There is joy.' She turned towards me, smiling, and it were a proper smile, not like all her other smiles; it actually went into her eyes. 'There is nothing better in the whole world than to love and be loved in return.'

I couldn't vouch for that. The only thing I knew were that love made people do daft things, terrible things.

'Love is when you'll do anything for someone, ain't it?' Like what I were doing now for Ma. Like what Ma had done for Pa. 'Like die for them.' Or kill for them, but I didn't say that.

'Yes,' she whispered.

'And what makes you love somebody?'

'There is no logic to it.'

'So we can love the wrong people? Like you loved Frank, and he were the wrong person?'

She scowled at me when I mentioned his name. Suddenly I wished to tell her what he were planning, that man what she loved the bones of, that man whose ring she polished and kept warm by her heart day and night. I wished to tell her that he were planning on doing her over and leaving the country with her money and a girl what she despised. I were building myself up to it as I were stroking the cat, and I promised that by the time I'd stroked all the way from the cat's head to the tip of its tail, I would say it, but she said something else first.

'I never knew my father.'

I'd lost my chance. She were staring through the window at the thin line of the sea on the horizon, and she weren't thinking of Frank no more.

'Not even his name,' she carried on. 'Hearn was the name of the man my mother married after I was born. For three years I was just Bonnie. All I know is that he came on a ship from some hot country, for my mother was as pale as you, and was gone on it again before the sun had risen.'

I wanted to tell her she were lucky to have never known him and the disappointment he'd no doubt bring, but really, when I thought about it properly, maybe she weren't very lucky; maybe I were luckier to have known Pa for them lovely ten years, after all.

'Do you think of him?' I said.

'Only when I look at the sea.'

'You'd like to find him?' Never before had I considered whether she'd had hopes and dreams for the future. The idea that she might were dreadful, knowing she'd never experience them.

'What would be the point? I might not like what I find. Sometimes it's better just to dream and leave it at that.'

I didn't know if she were playing me, if she'd all of a sudden got the ability to read my mind, but she were doing a good job of making me think about things. Maybe it would be better just to dream of killing her and getting my revenge?

Maybe we'd have all been so much better off if Pa had only dreamt of kissing her and had never actually done it.

'Bonnie, I think you're right. What you said before about being free. I should like to be free, Bonnie.'

I should have liked to have been free of all that pain and all that hate I'd felt for the last eight years. It were a weight what had been hanging round me, and no matter how hard I shook, it wouldn't ever come off.

She grabbed this notion with both hands and went on about how I should leave, take the money she'd offered, go and have a new life, find someone to love. She were getting a bit hysterical about it, and I knew then that she weren't looking forward to killing me any more than I were looking forward to killing her.

But I couldn't just let it go like that. If she'd have told me the truth I would have gone, swear it on that cat's life (well, I weren't going to swear it on my own seeing as mine didn't mean nothing to me). I just wanted to hear it from her and know the truth so that it would all make sense. I wanted to know she were sorry for what she'd done and everything what had gone wrong since. I wanted to know that she'd felt some of the pain too.

If she'd have done that, I'd have gone.

But she didn't.

CHAPTER 12

I'd waited around outside, pacing in and out of empty barns and talking to some farm dogs, wondering if I should go back to Bonnie and have it out with her, when I saw the landlord come running back. God, he were an ugly fellow, and bright red after tiring himself out. What had made him run so quick? What were he so eager to get back to? Bonnie, of course; I got sick just thinking of what she'd promised him and all the other promises she'd made to men like him.

So I walked to the beach. It were one of them empty sorts of places. There was no houses around, no promenades; it were just a great long stretch of sand, and the sea were far out. I sat in the dunes and played with the strands of grass and watched the sun set and the sky go from blue to navy to black. The moon were full and bright and shone over the landscape so that the water shimmered silver.

Then, in the darkness, I sobbed. I wept. I howled like a dog. There were no one around to hear me. I let everything go coursing out of me. I tore the grass out from its roots. I kicked the sand until my toes felt like they'd snapped. I cursed my pa. God, how I cursed him! I took the handkerchief out of my bag and spat on it and screwed it up under my shoe, and I were going to leave it there for the birds to shit on, but I just couldn't. Crying, I shoved it back inside my bag.

I curled up in all that sand grass, not caring for the bugs what might bite me or the night's cold what were making me shiver already, and I gazed out at the sky until my eyelids could not hold themselves up. When they fell, they stung as if they'd been scorched.

A murderer I would be. Bonnie had lost the chance to save herself; I would make her suffer twice over for how she'd lied to me. I would die the way my own pa had, and people could say it were his bad blood what ran through my veins if they so wished; I would go to the rope knowing justice had been done.

Seagulls woke me. The sky were just beginning to lighten, though there was clouds in it now, and the birds circled in the air shrieking at each other. I were as stiff as a plank, and the cold had fair on gone into my bones. My dress had that damp feeling to it what made my skin crawl as I struggled to sit up straight, and my joints creaked with every movement. There was shards of sleep and bits of grit in my eyes what I dug out with my fingernails, and I noticed the scent on my hands: the saltiness of the beach and the zing of the grasses.

My brain hurt. It had been dancing all night long with nightmares and memories and things what might happen. In the fog of all that pain, I knew there were only one thing I needed to do and that were get to Bonnie.

It took me a long time to walk back to the road. My legs would only go so fast no matter how much I wanted them to hurry. Eventually, I made it and said good morning to the cat on my way inside. It were licking blood off itself and there were a flurry of brown feathers floating in the breeze and lying on the grass by the hedgerow. The cat were looking real proud of itself. I winked at him.

In the inn, there were no one about. The table nearest the fireplace had dirty plates with bits of bread crusts on them and two wine glasses what was stained with drops of red. I did my best to tiptoe up the stairs and heard the landlord's snores, loud as a pig's, and then peeked into Bonnie's room. The curtains was open, the bed were made, and there were a silver trinket lying on her pillow. Bonnie were nowhere to be seen.

I ran downstairs, not caring for the noise I made. To warm me (for I'd be too slow if I had nothing in my belly), I gulped from a bottle of gin. It made me woozy for a moment so that I had to grip on to the bar to steady myself, but I were fine in a matter of seconds. I snatched the stale bread crusts off the plates, pushed them in my mouth, and set off on the road.

A coach came up behind me before I'd walked a hundred yards and God, were I glad for it. I fell inside that carriage as if I'd been running to Scotland and back and rested my face against the window so I could see our journey. I were sick with tiredness, but there were something inside me, like a bee had got into my guts, what were making me jumpy. My eyes was wide as I looked out for Bonnie. My face kept itching as if there were a cobweb over my flesh. My foot would not stop tapping itself.

And then the coach were slowing down, and I heard a woman's voice and the uneven sound of her steps on the road. The door opened and there were Bonnie, looking as if death had just caught up with her.

Bonnie got off a mile or so before Ulstone, saying it would be better for us not to be seen together. She were in a foul mood and so were I, but I thought I might as well not argue. She had a point, I admitted begrudgingly; it would be better if I weren't seen with a woman what might turn up dead in a day or two. I guessed she were thinking the same about me.

We went through a charade of prancing about like robbers, hiding behind trees and bushes as we crept to Frank's cottage. I were expecting him to be where I'd last left him, lying in bed and drinking away the morning, but the place were empty. And tidier than last time I'd been there – no clothes on the floor and no dirty cups what needed washing. It were cold compared to outside with no fires going, and in my shock, I just stood there as Bonnie said she'd check the smithy. While she were gone, I checked the house.

Some of his things was still there, as it turned out, like a jacket under the bed and some food in the cupboards, but the place were emptier than when I'd last been there. When I tried to open the chest to check the gold and silver, it were locked. I peeked through the keyhole, but it were too dark to see anything. I gave it a nudge with my shoe and it moved; it wouldn't have budged an inch if it had been full.

Maybe I were being set up after all. Maybe Frank had gone with the treasure, and now Bonnie would finish me off herself. She'd led me here because it would be easy to murder in a house so out of the way where nobody would hear me put up a fight. No one could trace her to Ulstone either. Maybe she'd dump me in a roadside ditch and leave my body to rot, and I'd get passed off as some mad girl what had drunk herself to death. Then she'd join Frank at the docks, and they'd sail away together, chuckling over how clever they'd been.

I had to take a seat in case I fell down.

'Not there,' she said, as she came back from the smithy.

'Where is he, Bonnie?'

'I don't know. He's gone. None of his things are here.'

'What's in the chest?' I wanted her to open it, but she were too smart and claimed ignorance.

'I think it must have come with the house,' she said. 'Probably something to do with the landlord.'

Silence. I didn't know what to say. I just sat there, dazed. All this time had passed, all this tension had built. I'd been waiting so long, and now I didn't know what to do.

'Fetch that firewood from outside, and we'll make some tea, shall we?'

I did as she said and set about stoking up the range while she found the tea and then went to get some water from the well. As she came back and set the kettle over the heat, I watched her go about her tasks and thought how lovely she looked in that cramped kitchen, like a flower in a patch of dirt.

I'd been a fool.

'Maybe he does,' I said, and I said it out loud though I hadn't meant to. *Maybe he does love her* were what I were thinking, but I managed to clasp my hands over my mouth before all of it escaped my lips. 'Where is he, Bonnie?'

'I already said, I don't know.'

'You sent him a note.'

She laughed as she poured the tea. 'I did not.'

'You sent the landlord with it yesterday. I know you did. Did you tell Frank to go? Did you tell him we was close?'

'You are being ridiculous.' I knew by the flush of her cheeks I were right.

'Why is he not here?' I think my fist hit the table. I were so confused, see. I thought I'd had it all planned out. I thought I'd get to Frank's and find him there with promises of love on his lips for me and a knife in his hand for Bonnie. But now everything were going wrong. I were losing my chance at revenge. I were losing it all. I had to get out of there. 'Maybe he's drinking.' I made for the door because there were this fear building in me that I were trapped and would never know fresh air again.

As I ran past Bonnie, something made a terrible ripping sound, and I looked down to find her with a fistful of my dress – Ma's dress. She'd torn it so that there were a gaping hole at my hip. My ma's dress, ruined. Like Bonnie always ruined everything.

'What've you done?'

She stood in front of the door, barring my way. 'You cannot go out like that now; they will think you mad.'

I surely were mad. I felt my body go hot, as if it were a match what had been struck, and I slammed her into that door and dug my hands into her soft flesh and squeezed until it felt like she might pop. God, how she trembled beneath me!

'You will go to the inn, and you will bring him here.' I gave her another shove, then tore my hands off her before they went for her throat. She ran away from me, and when her footsteps had faded in the distance, I punched that door with such force that the skin over one of my knuckles split.

But I hadn't the time to wallow. I grabbed my things and scarpered out of there before I understood what it was they'd been planning for me.

I ran out of the kitchen door and crashed straight into Frank.

It were like hitting a wall, and I fell back. He reached out to catch me, and I let out a scream because by now I were convinced that he were on Bonnie's side. He pushed his finger to my lips and pulled me into his chest. I couldn't move for fear, but then he kissed my head and stroked my cheek.

'You're all right,' he said as if he were speaking to a child what'd grazed their knee. 'Didn't mean to scare you.' He said it in whispers.

I turned on him. 'Where in God's name have you been?'

He found my anger amusing and folded his arms as if he were enjoying the spectacle I were making.

'We've been here getting on an hour now.'

'No you haven't. I saw you come.'

'What? You've been watching?'

''Course I have. Wanted to see what you'd do.'

He thought it were all a joke! That grin on his face were getting wider as I glowered at him. Did life matter so little to him that he thought this were all just some game?

'She thinks you've gone.'

'I know. She sent me a note telling me to leave the house.'

'Why?'

He shrugged. 'Lost her nerve, I suppose. Doesn't want to kill you.' He chuckled, then stopped. 'You haven't lost yours, have you?'

'No,' I said, shaking the doubts out of my head. 'No, I just thought maybe you had gone. That you did …'

'That I did what?'

I swallowed. 'Love her.'

That really made him laugh! He had to wipe the tears out his eyes. 'Go on and get inside. She'll be back before long.'

I did as he said because I were losing all ability to think clearly by that point. I sat on one of the chairs in the front room because it were darker in there and didn't hurt my head so much. He came in after a minute holding a hammer, tossing it from one hand to the other and smirking at me.

'What's that for?' I said.

'What do you think?'

I just stared at him for a moment. 'You can't.'

'Why not?'

He were seriously thinking of battering Bonnie to death!

'No. No, I won't let you.'

'Dead's dead, Lu.'

'I want to do it! I want to kill her. It's my revenge, Frank. It's up to me!' My voice had gone all high and loud, and I were finding it hard to get my breath.

He held the hammer up. 'All right, just calm down.'

'She's mine,' I said.

'Fine. I thought I'd spare you the trouble –'

The door opened.

Both of us froze. We didn't breathe. We just stared towards the kitchen and listened to Bonnie's heels on the tiles.

She came running at him and kissed him and told him I were a friend of hers from Stowmouth. Frank went along with it all as if it were a show and he were an actor. I couldn't play my part quite so well, but I did sigh with relief when he dropped that hammer and winked at me.

After a moment, she took him outside. I couldn't hear what they was saying and didn't want to neither, but when they came back in and Bonnie asked if I wanted tea, I could hear the glitch in her voice, the tremor of it, and knew she were scared.

Frank put her case in the bedroom as I pulled myself to my feet. As he passed me by the door he tried to catch my hand, but I moved around him before he managed it.

Bonnie were cleaning off the table and having a bit of a tidy, but I saw the shaking of her hands as she did so and wondered what exactly had passed between her and Frank outside. She were not the same in his presence; she seemed smaller, less sure of herself. She started to hum as I set my own bag on the table, and the sound of it brought me up short.

'What is that tune?' I said, because I couldn't think of the name of it; my mind were filled with my ma holding me tight and rocking me in her arms as sunlight made her hair look like she were an angel.

'Just something my mother used to sing.'

'Mine too.'

When I looked at Bonnie again, her eyes was wet.

'Do you know the words?' she said.

I started to sing them, surprised at how strong my memories was, and my voice quivered as I tried to stop myself from crying. Bonnie spoke over me before I lost myself completely. 'Time for tea.'

I swallowed my tears down as she poured the drinks. Now were the time I had been waiting for …

'Where's your flask?' I said.

'In my case.'

'Go and get it then.'

She did as I said. I had a matter of seconds, but I were ready. I took the cup what she'd drunk from before and tipped half of the tea down the sink. I opened my bag and snatched my own flask out, and then I poured what were inside it into her cup, right to the top. The flask were in my bag, and my bag were shut again before she returned.

'This is yours.' I slid her cup towards her. She didn't look at it twice. 'Which one for Frank?'

She pointed at one of the almost identical cups – the one which had a tiny chip on the handle, invisible to anyone what hadn't looked so hard at it – and into that, I poured the fly-paper water from her flask. I sniffed it, just to make sure it had no smell.

'Half a cup won't be enough,' she said. She were biting her lip again. 'He'd need all of it to kill him.'

'Then we'll make another pot after this one.' I put more water into the kettle and set it over the heat.

'I best give it to him. He'll think it strange if you serve him.'

I turned towards her and saw her smiling at me – that terrible smile of hers – with two cups in her hands. There were one cup left on the table for me. She watched me take it, and still she smiled.

The cup with the chipped handle.

YOU KNOW how it went from there. Frank wound both of us up, and Bonnie drank all of her tea without suspecting a thing.

It didn't take as long as I were expecting. Grandma didn't drop off for almost an hour when she took her medicine, but I supposed that were because Grandma were used to it. Bonnie were gone in a matter of minutes, but for all them minutes as she sipped, I don't think I took in a single breath. My eyes was fixed on her as she went drowsier and drowsier and slumped further into her chair, and when the cup fell out her hand and smashed, by God, my heart did pound!

Frank and me just stared at her for a while, seeing if she'd start up again. She didn't.

'Is she dead?' Frank said and gave her a prod with his finger.

'Sleeping.' I could just see the slight rise and fall of her chest as her chin rested on it.

'Best do it quick. How will you …'

'You have some rope?'

He faltered for a moment. Really, he were paling at the thought of strangling her, when he'd happily have hammered the life out of her! He looked away from Bonnie as if he suddenly had a conscience. 'What a business.' He shook his head.

'Did you think I were playing, Frank? Did you think this were all a game?'

'No. No, it's just' – he nodded at Bonnie's still body – 'I don't know. We've known each other a long time.'

I could have struck him. All that pomp and bluster, and now he were getting scared.

He went to sip his tea.

'Don't.'

He stopped, the cup an inch from his lips, and raised his brows at me.

'It's poisoned.'

He stared at the tea in horror. 'Christ, Lu! I've already had some!'

'It's fine.' I put a hand on his shoulder to calm him. 'A sip won't do anything to a man like you.' I took the cup from him and chucked the tea on to the ashes. 'Here, have mine instead.'

I rubbed his back as he took it from me and drank. He drank it all.

'Thirsty business,' he said, with a nervous laugh.

'Another cup?'

He nodded. Both of us had our faces turned from Bonnie.

'Move her on to the bed and go and fetch that rope.' I kissed him on the forehead. 'I'll make you some more tea.'

CHAPTER 13

The rope lay twisted on the table. A good thick rope, one I could wrap my hands round and get a good grip on.

But do you think I could move? I sat there on that bench as Frank paced around me, taking gulps of his third cup of tea as the minutes turned into hours and the afternoon ran on.

'I don't like this, Lu. What's all this waiting around for? Turning my insides up.'

I could hear his stomach over his footsteps. It were tumbling, and there were a shine on his forehead what were getting worse by the minute.

'I won't kill her in the daylight.'

'Christ! We'll be here hours.'

'You got somewhere to be?'

'Yes. We've got somewhere to be, remember? The docks. The boat!' He were getting all bitter and agitated. 'We've got to get her to the woods, too.'

'The woods?'

He sat beside me and put a fist through his hair. 'What else do you think we'd do with the body?'

'Why the woods?'

'We take her in deep enough and no one'll find her for weeks, if ever. And if they do, it'll just look like an attack, some man had his way with her. That's if the animals don't get her.'

I frowned at my hands on the rope. Nothing he said made sense.

'We discussed this before. We can't leave her here in my house, can we?'

I shook my head to please him, to shut him up.

He drank his tea, and his hand were quaking as he did so. He slammed the cup on the table. 'I need something stronger.'

There were a half-empty bottle of rum he found in one of the cupboards, and he gulped that down without offering any of it to me.

'You didn't tell me you was married.'

He wiped his wet lips on the back of his hand. 'It was just a daft thing we did when we were young. It doesn't mean anything.'

'It means something to her. She keeps the ring by her heart.'

'Aye, Bonnie would make sure she got herself a nice bit of gold.' He leant over the table, suddenly quiet, and his lips was working so that he looked like there was something stuck between his teeth what he couldn't get out. Then he were up and dashing for the door, and he were sick in the bushes. He couldn't straighten his back for a while. He stood there with his hands pressing into his knees and breathing deep and looking like it were the hardest thing in the world to do.

'Come inside and sit down. It's your nerves and that rum what's done that to you.'

'My nerves are fine,' he mumbled as he staggered inside. He looked awful; his skin were grey as ash, and he were starting to shiver.

'Sit yourself down, and I'll make more tea.'

'I'd be fine if you'd just have done with her and we could be on our way.' He trudged into the next room, but he did as I'd told him. I boiled the kettle and made the tea and poured the very last trickle of the fly-paper water into his cup.

THE DAY DRAGGED ON. Frank got worse. His breathing were quicker than usual, and he kept having to run out the door and for the privy, though sometimes he didn't make it.

He were weakening now as the rain poured down. How it thrashed on that roof! You'd have thought God were pelting stones at us. When Frank spoke, I couldn't hear him over the noise. Not that I wanted to – anything to drown out his moaning and his accusations.

'It's that bit of tea you let me drink,' he said more than once and scowled at me as his teeth chattered. 'Fucking bitch,' he said, but I couldn't tell whether he were saying this about me or Bonnie.

But as the rainclouds blacked out the sky, and night came and I had to light a candle so I could see further than an inch from my face, he stopped saying anything. He curled up on that wooden chair with his winter coat over him and closed his eyes. Every now and then his body would buckle, and he'd need to empty one of his ends. Half the time he didn't manage to get to the bucket I'd brought in for him and there'd be stains seeping from his trousers and splatters all over the tiles. Dear God, the stench in there were enough to kill you!

'She really loved you,' I said to him in one of his quieter times. The rain and the wind made the ashes in the grate blow up and move about as if they was the ashes of some haunted soul. 'She would have done anything for you.'

I left him there shivering. I hoped my words had meant something to him, but I doubted it; he were too far gone by then.

With the rope in one hand and a candle in the other, I went to the bedroom, peeked through the gap to see what state she were in, then crept inside.

The smell weren't too bad in there, and the rain didn't seem quite so loud, though it scratched on the windows worse than it did in the front room. He'd laid Bonnie down on her back with her head at a funny angle, and her arm had fallen off the mattress and looked as if it were broken. The gale through the window frames made strands of her hair swirl about her face.

I set the candle on the side and went to put her straight. As I touched her skin, I gasped at how cold she were. Dead. I'd given her too much of Grandma's medicine, and she'd died in her sleep. Died peacefully.

I pinched myself for my stupidity, but inside me, there were something like relief. I wouldn't have to strangle her after all.

I sat on the bed. I were trying to work out what I should do next. I'd been so set on taking the rope to her that I hadn't thought what I'd do afterwards. I were trying to get things clear in my mind when there came a little murmur. The faintest movement of her lips, a flickering of her eyelids. She weren't dead after all.

My second chance for revenge, though it weren't as sweet as I'd been expecting.

I stood up, pulled the rope taut between my hands. I lifted her head and slid the rope underneath her neck. I straddled her, taking care not to tear her dress, and grabbed the opposite ends of the rope.

Pull. Just pull, I said to myself as I stared at her.

Not a muscle had moved in her face; she were sleeping soundly, without nightmares, like a child sleeps. The candlelight struck her chain which were bunched around her neck underneath the rope. I tugged the ring out from under her dress and held it in my palm. I felt the heat of the gold on my skin and saw how the edges of it had smoothed down over the years from how much she'd caressed and kissed it.

I couldn't do it.

I dropped the rope. I dropped the ring, and it bounced against her breast. I jumped away and cursed her and took my own locket into my hands and wept. Everything she'd done to me and my own, and now my tenderness were getting in the way of justice! My fingernails pierced the skin on my palms before I felt the pain.

Foolish girl!

I gripped the rope again and paced back and forth before Bonnie, urging myself to be strong. It burned my hands as I twisted it, but each time I lurched for her, I tore myself away before I could do any harm.

I charged out of there, slamming the door behind me. Back in the foulness of the front room, Frank shivered under his coat. He raised his head to glance at me.

'Is it done?' he whispered, and I barely heard him.

All I saw were him earlier, that wicked grin on his face as Bonnie cowered beside him. All I heard was his taunts and his mocking laughter about a woman what'd only ever spoken about him with love. All I felt was his hands on my skin and the pleasure he took from having me.

The rope were tight in my hands, and without thinking too hard about it, I marched over to him, went behind his chair, tossed the rope over his head and into the hollow of his neck, and I pulled back hard. I were so fast he didn't have time to do anything.

I pulled until his head were sliding over the back of his chair. His hands fought against the rope. His body twisted as he tried to get away from me. No matter how hard he struggled, nothing were going to stop me.

I dragged on that rope with all my strength. My arms trembled. Still, Frank carried on jerking, his feet slipping on his own shit on the tiles as he failed to get sure footing. Did I let go? Did I heck! I held on to that rope until he'd lost his fight, until his face had gone purple and his tongue stuck out all fat from his mouth and his eyes bulged from their sockets. Until he looked just like my pa had looked when he'd finally gone still on the end of that noose.

AFTER, I had to sit down. I were panting and sweating as I made my way into the kitchen. The rain had started to ease off, and in the sky, the clouds was breaking and skidding along so fast that moonlight flashed on and off. I sipped the dregs of my tea to moisten my dry mouth, and once my hands had stopped shaking, I gathered my things and walked out the back door.

The earth had that smell to it of rain in the summer night. Leaves had been beaten off their branches and lay soggy on the ground. The wind were sharp, and the trees in the woods behind me yawned and whispered amongst themselves.

There were only one road in and out of Ulstone, and so I walked it quick and went north. The houses was dark at the windows, but the inn were alive, and men's ruddy faces laughed and jeered behind the glass, though they never looked outside. I ran past the last few houses with the church looming up ahead and didn't slow until there was only hedges about me and the noise of animals.

I kept walking. A little while later, I heard the distant tolling of Ulstone's bells what told me it were eleven o'clock, and with each step I put between Frank and Bonnie and myself, the easier I could breathe.

What did I have in my head, you might be thinking? I hadn't had the nerve to strangle Bonnie, but I would see her dead. Folk had seen her that day asking after Frank. Frank were dead in his house. Bonnie's things was everywhere. I didn't imagine that a blacksmith could go too long in a place like that without being needed, and when people went looking, they'd find him there dead. I'd wait for the law to serve the justice it had failed to give eight years ago.

I were convincing myself of this as I walked, how it were the best thing to do. I kept saying it over and over to myself. I stopped to open my locket and take out the curl of Ma's hair and brush it over my cheek, hoping it would give me some comfort or bring her voice to me on the wind, but it didn't. I closed the locket and tucked it inside my dress and carried on walking.

I tried shaking out thoughts of Bonnie waking to find her beloved Frank dead and reeking with his own shit and sick and her being forced to the gallows for the crowds to ogle and jeer at. She'd draw in the people, that would be certain. They'd call it a holiday to come and see her swing, see her beautiful body gnash at the noose before it were cut down and taken to the doctors and their knives.

I would not think about it. I concentrated on the rhythm of my strides. Once or twice, something shot out of the hedgerows beside me and gave me a start, but they was nothing but rats or weasels. And then, on the horizon, there came some black sets of buildings and the faint pricks of candlelight. I'd reached another village.

Like Ulstone, this one were small, and most folk were sleeping inside their homes. This village had a public house too, though it weren't as big as Ulstone's inn. Men's voices pounded through the walls and echoed in the empty road.

Outside the door, in the pool of a streetlamp, a dog slept as it waited for its master. I were smiling at the sight of this dog, so peaceful and innocent as it lay there, not understanding a thing about grief and hate, when the pub door opened. The dog lifted its head, made a quick dive out of the drunkard's way, and kept its eyes on the man as if it didn't trust him.

The man staggered out. Cries followed him, and the door were slammed on him; he were no longer welcome, so it seemed. He cursed at the door and then began to fiddle with himself down there until I saw his private part pop out from his trousers; he were peeing against the door! Wobbling, he peed all up and down and side to side, then shook himself, folded himself back inside his trousers, and smiled as if he'd done an honest day's work. Then he stumbled towards the road.

I'd been keeping to the shadows, but he were heading straight for me. I needed to move. I started to run but he saw me. He shouted something what were indecipherable, and then his boots was stomping up behind me. He were quick for a drunk! My legs didn't seem to be working very well though; I'd lost most of my strength tugging on that rope.

'Lucy!' He were right behind me. His hand came to my shoulder and spun me round. I were ready to slash at him but found him to be smiling. The moonlight put a mad twinkle in his eyes. 'Lucy, isn't it? Lovely little Lucy.'

I fought through my brain and the memories until I recognised his face. 'Paul Meadows.'

'That's right. Well done. You're the one who gave me this.' He pointed to his right eye, and I could just make out the faint cut on his eyebrow and the smudge of a bruise. He blew out a long breath because the run had made him pant, and he wiped his forehead with his sleeve. 'Not that I blame you. Always causing trouble, I am.'

'So I see.' I kept glancing behind him to make sure no one

had followed him out. They hadn't. 'You ain't got far since last I saw you.'

'Walked most of it. Thought it would do me good.' He laughed heartily. 'Neither have you, so it seems. How is your beautiful Miss Dayton?' He leant forward conspiratorially and winked, and I smelt the beer on him.

'Sleeping.' It weren't really a lie.

He nodded, and after looking about himself – trying to remember where he were, so I thought – he turned back to me with a frown as the village's church bells struck midnight. 'You're out late. Meeting an admirer?'

'No.' I began to walk away from him, but he kept step beside me.

'Does your Miss Dayton know where you are?'

I didn't answer him. I hoped he'd be like any other animal and go away when he got bored.

'So this is north, is it? This is where you were heading?'

I clamped my arms across myself and tried to hurry. He giggled and trotted beside me.

'You'll make me ill, all this running after you.'

'Then stop.'

'Oh, come on, Lucy. Lucy!' He grabbed my arm, and I swung round and landed a punch on his left eye this time. He fell back clutching his face, though it hadn't been a hard punch, and when he stood up again there weren't a mark on him.

'It's all right,' he said breathlessly, 'I won't hurt you, Lucy. I … I'm sorry, for what I did to your Miss Dayton. It was wrong of me.' He sighed and dropped his head back so he were looking up at the sky as if he were suddenly exhausted. 'I can't help it sometimes.'

'You should keep your hands to yourself.'

He nodded, then dropped to his knees and sat on the road, worn out. 'I don't blame you for what you did to me.'

'Neither do I,' I said, glaring down at him. 'And you should be ashamed for pissing on that pub door.'

'Oh, they deserved it.' He winked at me. 'You are a fierce little thing, aren't you? I bet Miss Dayton counted her lucky stars when she found you to protect her.'

I turned from him. He couldn't have been more wrong.

'I really am sorry to have frightened her like I did. I can't remember too much but I ... well, I remember bits of it. I remember her screams. I remember you shouting at me to let go of her. You're like her little guard dog, aren't you?'

He tugged the hem of my frock, and I thought he were going to try and go for me like he'd gone for Bonnie, but he were just frowning and looking sad. 'Your gown is torn, Lucy. I could fix it for you if you like? I could make you a new one?'

'No, thank you.' I pulled my dress out of his hands.

He dragged himself to his feet, wobbled for a moment before finding his balance, and blinked the stars out of his eyes.

'Give my sincere apologies to your mistress, won't you, Lucy? I do so hope I have not harmed her in any way. Really, I never meant to. We've all done things we never meant to, haven't we? But I'm not a bad man, Lucy. You understand? Underneath all the shit, I'm not a bad man.'

He turned towards the village, his shoes scuffing on the road as he struggled to walk. 'Perhaps we might meet on the road again sometime? I should like to make you both new dresses, two new dresses of emerald green for you and your mistress ... emerald green ...' He went off singing to himself about dresses and what-not. I watched him until he'd gone out of sight.

I stood there on that black road, and half of my body were pulled one way and the other half the other.

If I hadn't seen that awful man! If he hadn't made me think, made me remember, made me sorry …

Damn him and his drink! Damn me and my conscience! Damn Bonnie!

I stalked back to Ulstone as the night stole away my time.

CHAPTER 14

It were after one in the morning when Ulstone come up before me. The place were truly dark now with nothing stirring at all, or nothing what I could see, anyway.

I waited on the edge of the village, wondering if I really did want to do this – return to Frank's house. It wouldn't be pleasant. But Bonnie were in there, and she'd be scared when she woke, and no matter how much I told myself I hated her, the thought of her in pain were not as enjoyable to me as it should have been.

So I walked on until I saw Frank's house behind the grey bushes and the yellow glow of a candle through the window. I crept round to the back and pushed open the door, trying to be quiet, but of course, the door stuck on the kitchen tiles and made a screech.

My empty cup were on the kitchen table where I'd left it. The fire in the range were almost out. The smell of Frank's shit made me put a hand to my mouth. And then, just one of them feelings, you know, like someone watching you.

Holding my breath, I tiptoed towards the next room.

Bonnie were in there, on her hands and knees by Frank's corpse. Her sleeves was pushed up to her elbows. There were a bucket of foul water beside her and an old towel in her hands what was brown, and her mauve dress were darkened here and there with water or something worse. She leant back and rested on her ankles, sighed, and brushed her hair out of her face.

'I knew it would be a bad death,' she said without turning towards me. 'Didn't know it would smell so awful though.' She dunked the towel in the bucket, wrung it out, and wiped the tiles. 'It was supposed to be you.'

'I know.'

She nodded sadly, then pointed at Frank. 'It was probably for the best. The rope, I mean. More merciful.'

'Don't know about that.' I went further into the room. The rope was draped over Frank's body, and there was clear bruises round his neck. 'Didn't mean for it to be.'

She flinched, breathed in shakily. 'Where have you been?'

'I were leaving you.'

She dunked the towel again. 'Where were you going?'

I shrugged. Honestly, I didn't know. I would have walked until my feet had been ribbons.

I slumped onto the chair. 'I were going to hang you, you know. I were going to let Frank die from the arsenic. I assumed someone would find you both and think you'd poisoned him and killed yourself. Poison is a woman's weapon, ain't it?'

A faint smile passed over her face. 'What happened?'

Again, I shrugged; I weren't prepared to tell her I'd gone soft. 'I couldn't do it. So I left you here. I thought the police might say you killed Frank, and they'd hang you instead.'

Not a glimmer of shock could be found in her features. Perhaps she'd known all along that I were evil.

'Why did you come back?'

'God knows.'

She dropped the towel in her bucket. On top of her chair were one of Frank's old shirts. She got to her feet stiffly, swayed slightly, then pushed the shirt over the floor with her foot to take up the brown water. Unsteadily, she lifted the bucket and hobbled outside with it. I heard the gush of water as she threw it into the privy. She came inside again and went to the bedroom. There were the snagging and tearing of material, puffing and panting, and in a few moments she came through in her old blue gown with her hair tied back with a plain ribbon. She sat down. Frank were between us.

'He suffered,' I said.

She looked at her dirty hands what lay in her lap and picked at her nails.

'He would've let you die, Bonnie.'

'No,' she breathed.

'He would have let me kill you. He would have let you suffer so he could have me.' She winced, so I kept chipping away. 'He wanted to go to America with me. He said he had enough money for us to live like kings. He didn't love you. He said he hadn't love you for years –'

'All right!' She sighed, bit her lip. 'I believe you.'

My cheeks flamed. I dropped my gaze to the floor. What were I becoming? I'd never been so mean.

'What was it like?' she whispered. 'Was he gentle?'

'I don't understand.'

'When he made love to you.' She looked at me, but there didn't seem to be any malice in her. 'You were the widow, weren't you?'

There were no point trying to deny it. Again, heat scalded my face when I thought of the depths I'd sunk to for revenge. 'Yes. He were gentle with me. He were kind.'

She sniffed. She looked sadder now than she had done when I'd told her he'd plotted to murder her.

'We never …'

I waited, but she sucked her lips like she were holding her words in.

'You never what?'

She cleared her throat. 'Tickled.'

I think my jaw must have dropped. I almost laughed because it were such an unbelievable notion, yet she were so defeated, so shrivelled and small, that I couldn't see why she'd lie. 'Why?'

Her fingers fluttered towards him as if she would touch his arm, but she stopped before she reached him. 'It were only ever a weapon, something I could use against somebody to get what I wanted from them. I never did it with Frank because I loved him, and it never meant love to me. I didn't realise it meant so much to him.'

'He's a man.' I didn't know if I believed what I had been told; I hoped I were wrong about men. I said it more as a way to console her.

'I suppose I should have known. Things were never the same with us since Bridgefield.'

Nothing had ever been the same since they'd gone to Bridgefield. If only they'd never walked across that bridge. If only she'd chosen someone other than Mrs Campbell.

We sat there, thinking the same sorts of things, no doubt. What both of us would have given to have never laid eyes on each other.

'I thought I'd seen it wrong after Pa died,' I whispered. Now was the time to explain, to tell the truth. Neither of us could hide any longer.

'All them little touches, them little kisses; I didn't understand them at the time, I just knew something weren't right. But after he died, I couldn't bear to think he were capable of such a thing. Not when he'd had my ma at home, waiting for him. So I convinced myself that I'd been wrong.'

I opened my bag and took out the handkerchief. 'I hadn't seen this in years. You never asked about my ma, Bonnie. Did you feel too guilty about her?'

She shrugged, but her eyes was misting up.

'She were so sad after Pa had gone. She never smiled, and she were always smiling before. She lasted five years until it were too much, and then she walked herself down to the bridge in her black mourning dress and threw herself into the river.'

Bonnie blinked, and a tear spilled onto her cheek.

'Someone saved her. Grandma were ashamed. First Ma were the wife of a murderer, then she were sinning again by trying to kill herself. Grandma got her changed out of that gown and put her in this one' – I gestured at what I were wearing – 'and then sent her away. Three years Ma were in the asylum until she finished herself not two weeks ago. I went to see her and, you know, she looked so pretty again. I think she'd gone back to Pa. It were like she were smiling.

'Anyway,' I said, and sniffed because I had to be strong to say all this; I weren't going to start crying before I got to the truth of it all. 'I got her things what she'd had with her when they took her to that place. Her dress, her shoes, her bonnet, this locket, and this handkerchief.' I held it up before me. Bonnie couldn't look at it. 'And then I knew that I'd been right, that what I'd seen really had happened. That Pa had really done that to Ma, to us.

'Pa loved this handkerchief, you see. He kept it in his pocket close to his chest, and he'd hold it to his face sometimes and smile, and he never blew his nose on it or nothing like that. His name stitched so beautifully … stitched by someone he loved and given as a gift. Stitched by you, Bonnie.'

She shook her head, and another tear dislodged from the rim of her eye.

'Yes, Bonnie. I know it were you because my ma had never learnt to read or write. She were only the daughter of a washerwoman, see, though she were the prettiest girl in the town. Any boy would have married her just for her sweet face, but it were Pa what got her. They was the happiest man and wife in all of Bridgefield. Until you came along.'

'I'm sorry,' she whispered.

'What were so special about you? Why did he want you?'

She shrugged. 'I was different.'

Such a simple answer, and I knew it to be true. How fickle we all were!

'I know you killed Nicholas Campbell, Bonnie.'

She didn't deny it. Her chin sunk onto her chest, and she closed her eyes.

'Tell me what happened.'

She took in a long, deep breath, and when it came out of her, it juddered and made her whole body shake.

'Your father was sacked by Nicholas for fiddling the books. You didn't see any of the money from it because it all went to me. He was fiddling the books for me.' She smiled briefly. 'He was a nice man, your father. He was handsome and kind, and he really loved you, Luella.'

'Don't.' I didn't want to hear it.

'He did. I know you hate him, but he did love you, and he loved your mother too.'

'Then why did he –'

'Don't we all do foolish things?'

That brought me up short. But to explain it as foolish didn't do it justice.

'I was devastated when he was sacked because it would make things harder for me. It was easy money. And then Nicholas was there all of the time, and it was almost impossible to take anything without him noticing.' She sucked her lips over her teeth and bit at a flake of dry skin.

'Frank and I were due to leave that night. There was no point in us being there any longer. I had gone into the study for a last look round to see what we could take with us, and Nicholas caught me. I know what I did was wrong, Luella, but that man was evil. He attacked me, not in the way I said before; he beat me. He threw me from wall to wall, calling me all sorts of vile names. For a moment, I thought I was going to die, but then he threw me against the mantelpiece, and I found a fire poker. When he came for me again, I hit him with it. He went down immediately.'

She clutched her hands together in her lap. I wished they'd been clean; the sight of them covered in dirt like that were making me uneasy.

'Frank came. He'd heard some of the commotion. He checked to see if I was hurt. I told him I had a plan to fix things. I told him not to worry. And he didn't.'

'You went for Pa.'

She nodded. 'I went to his house and got him.'

'I know. I heard you at the door, and I followed you back.' That did surprise her.

'What did you see?'

'Frank running away. I saw you, shaking and crying. I waited behind the trees as you and Pa went inside.'

'Your father was only protecting me.' I could see the working of her jaw as she ground her teeth. 'Not just me.' Her hands rose to rest on her stomach. 'I said I was pregnant. I said the child was his.'

You know when you think you haven't heard something right because it just don't make sense? That's how I were feeling. I couldn't speak.

'That's why he died for me, Luella.'

She closed her eyes. I just sat there and thought of Bonnie with a baby; it were impossible.

I made my voice work. 'He gave himself up to save the baby.'

She nodded.

'You never had a child, did you?'

She shook her head.

I didn't know what to say. So long I'd thought him a fool, a villain for what he did to Ma. He still were, in a way, but now I could understand him a bit more. My pa would never have let his own flesh and blood die.

I should have hated Bonnie. I should have run at her and clawed her skin off her face. But you know what? All I could think about were what an awful mess everything were. What a sad, painful mess everything had turned out to be.

'I'm sorry,' Bonnie whispered, and I think, probably for the first time in her whole life, she meant it.

I PASSED SOME MINUTES CRYING. It were one of them tired cries, when you don't make a sound, and the tears just roll down your cheeks because you haven't the strength to wipe them away.

Bonnie said nothing. She didn't try to comfort me or defend her actions, and I were grateful for the silence because in the quiet, I could remember Pa.

I remembered him being led to the scaffold, his hands bound behind his back, his head down and his face calm as everyone shouted at him. It weren't a friendly crowd. Killing Nicholas Campbell had put the carpet factory in trouble, and the staff was out and showing their anger. But Pa didn't take no notice of what he got called, and his legs didn't shake as he mounted the steps, and he didn't baulk at the sight of the noose what were waiting for him.

He didn't wish to speak any last words. He refused the cap. I remembered Ma sobbing all the time and how she crushed my hand as she held it tight. She'd told me not to come, but she hadn't had the strength to stop me. She'd told me not to watch, but she didn't take her eyes off Pa to know that I too couldn't look away.

When the noose were slipped over his head and the knot brought under his ear, he searched the crowd and found us. It were the first time I'd ever seen him scared. His eyes watered, his chin wobbled, and Ma shouted out his name and that she loved him. A sob escaped from him, and he lowered his head as if he were too ashamed to look at us.

That were the last time I met my pa's gaze.

When he lifted his chin next time, he were searching for something else. When he found it, the frown fell off his face, his tears dried, and he nodded once. I followed his gaze and saw Bonnie stood amidst the townsfolk in her silk gown with a bonnet pulled close to her face to protect her from the rain. I scowled at her, hating the beauty of her, when the crowd gasped and Ma screamed. When I faced Pa again, he were several inches lower than where he'd been before. His face were turning red and his eyes was popping out and he were jerking around in mid-air.

I hadn't known then that the hangman were being merciful when he'd pulled on Pa's legs. I'd started to scream as Pa went redder and redder and then purple. His face had puffed up as the hangman dragged him down with all his strength. I'd shouted with the crowd for the hangman to let off him, and at one point, I prised myself out of Ma's grip and went charging for the scaffold ready to beat that man off my pa, but folk had stopped me and wrestled me back to Ma.

We was at Grandma's that night. I never saw Pa or Mrs Campbell ever again.

I were never a child again.

CHAPTER 15

We made an awful sound, grunting and panting, as we dragged Frank through the woods. Several times we fell over and went splattering into the undergrowth. Our clothes tore on branches; our skin ripped on brambles; our hair got snagged out of its roots. We sounded like sailors for all our cursing. Frank were over a head taller than both of us and weighed something shocking, and we needed to take him far enough into them trees so there were little chance of anyone finding him any time soon.

God knows how long we struggled. The leaves was so thick they blocked out any moonlight, so we was working in near on pitch black most of the time. But in the end, we got to a section thick with trees and bushes, and the ground beneath our feet felt spongy and soft, and as we dragged him along some more, my foot went squelching straight into some water.

'Wait!' I went on all fours and fumbled around in the darkness. My hands was covered in icy water, and I crawled into it further, feeling it get deeper and deeper; it were coming up to my elbows and then to my shoulders. It smelt stagnant, and I dreaded to think what were in there, but there were a cover of blown leaves on its surface, and I thought if we could get Frank's body into it properly so that the water covered him, then the leaves would hide him even better.

'Put him in here.' I grabbed the shoulders of his jacket and pulled, while Bonnie pushed at the other end.

We worked by listening, and we heard his body slither over the wet dirt and then the water splash and lap at him. After a few more shoves, I ran my hands over him and were fair on certain that he were submerged. I kicked leaves and dragged twigs on top of him nevertheless, just to be on the safe side, and then both of us lay back on top of that soggy forest floor and rested.

Things moved and scurried all around us. I felt something like a spider's web fall over my forehead but didn't brush it off. My hands and feet was beginning to tingle with the cold from the water, though the rest of me were sweating, and I could feel Bonnie's heat buzzing off her as she lay beside me.

'Sorry,' I whispered once my breath were back to normal. 'For Frank.'

She didn't say anything, but I'd seen the pain on her face earlier when we'd talked about what we had to do with his body and the way she looked at him when she knew she'd never be able to visit his grave. I'd felt a bit of triumph knowing that I'd hurt her like she'd hurt me, but the feeling had been only fleeting.

'I should have told you the truth when you asked for it,' Bonnie said, and I could hear the regret in her voice.

I wondered what I'd have really done if she'd told me the truth at the inn when I'd asked for it. Would I have gone away as I'd promised? I liked to think I would have. Maybe I'd have been halfway across the ocean by now. Maybe

Bonnie would have never known Frank's disloyalty. Maybe I wouldn't have had a man's blood on my hands and be damned for eternity.

'Come on.' I felt for her arm and pulled her up. 'We need to get back and get going before the light comes.'

WE MANAGED to find our way out them woods (God knows how, more by luck than judgement) and got back to the house. We was in such a mess! Torn and bleeding and drowning in muck. We washed each other with water from the well and brushed each other's hair and helped each other into clean dresses (Bonnie gave me one of hers seeing as I had no other). She put her ring next to her heart, and I put my locket next to mine, and neither of us said a word to the other about it.

We found the lock to the chest in a set of drawers in the bedroom along with roughly one hundred pounds in notes. Frank had taken lots of the trinkets and sold them, so it seemed, as when we opened the chest half of the stuff were gone.

Bonnie split the money between us, then started stuffing the rest of the trinkets in her bag. It were as she were doing this and coming to the bottom of the chest when I saw something familiar: a pretty china saucer with gilt on the edges. It were Mrs Campbell's, what I'd seen her pour milk into so many times to give to her kittens in the barn. And then a silver teapot what she'd made tea for me in. And a hand mirror what had roses painted on the back of it. A gold thimble what had a pattern of flowers round the base of it, the petals filled in with turquoise stones. A cake knife, a few necklaces of gold and diamonds and pearls, some silk gloves, a ring with a ruby set into it.

Every piece held some memory of Mrs Campbell. How she'd been robbed!

Bonnie took particular care of not looking at me, and I couldn't bring myself to speak to her for a while. I wrapped Mrs Campbell's things in a bedsheet and carefully packed them into my bag. Bonnie didn't try to stop me. She offered me more of the stolen items, but I didn't want them. I weren't taking Mrs Campbell's stuff for the price of it; I were taking it so I could keep a part of her with me forever.

Bonnie couldn't fit all of the trinkets into her bag. She made sure the stuff she left were the cheapest and the sort what wouldn't be recognised as belonging to anyone in particular. We did a last run round the house making sure no trace of us remained, and then we blew out the candle and headed for the road. Bonnie looked back once, and I thought she might have cried a little, but she didn't.

We walked for hours as the next day started up all around us. We was both a bit on edge, and could you blame us? We hopped on a stagecoach for the last few miles into the city and didn't say a word to each other until it stopped in Bristol.

Bonnie opened the door, but I didn't move.

'What are you doing?' she said. Outside the coach, the noise of the city were loud. 'We best hurry.'

'I ain't going to America.'

She frowned, then shut the door so we was back in the quiet, just the two of us. 'What do you mean? We have to.'

'You have to, Bonnie. No one saw me.' I didn't mean it to sound nasty, I were just being honest. 'I don't want to go.'

'I thought you weren't going back to Bridgefield?'

'I ain't.'

'Then where?'

I shrugged. 'North.'

She smiled. 'No point in breaking a habit.'

I nodded, returned her smile.

'I thought we were going to go together?'

'I don't think that's for the best,' I said. 'We wouldn't last long cooped up in a boat for weeks on end. I'd probably push you overboard.'

She laughed. It were a very real possibility.

'You're probably right.' She glanced out of the window and sighed. 'We both need a fresh start. And I'm looking forward to being on the sea.'

'I know.' She were itching for it, I could tell. 'Promise me, Bonnie, that you won't do what you did here.' I meant about her stealing from the ladies, of course, but I didn't put it into words in case there was any spies around.

'I'll try.'

The coach moved; the driver were climbing onto his seat. Bonnie opened the door.

'You're a good person, Luella.'

'I'm a –' I couldn't say the word out loud. *Murderer.* No matter how much I tried to justify his death, Frank's words kept spiralling round in my mind: *What would that make you, Luella? You'd be worse than me.*

She squeezed my hand. 'We both are,' she said, and somehow it were a comfort to me. 'And your father was a good man, remember that. Don't hate him. Hate does no one any good.'

She dismounted and turned to me one last time. 'Good-bye, Luella.'

Then she smiled that beautiful smile of hers and strode off for the docks.

CHAPTER 16

I'd never had any intention of sailing to America. It weren't a new world what I wanted, it were an old one, but that were impossible.

I went north, as I said I would. And then I went east so that when I looked out at the sea, I wouldn't have to think of Bonnie across the water and what kind of life she might have been living.

I never heard if they found Frank's body. As the days turned into weeks and the weeks into months and the months into years, I always watched out for news of it in the papers, but I never saw nothing. That didn't mean I stopped worrying about it. I had new nightmares from then on, and in every one of them Frank came back to haunt me. He dragged me to the scaffold and put the noose round my neck, and I looked down to see Bonnie smiling at me. I woke each time with such a sweat on that I had to get out of bed and stand outside for a bit, even in the winter.

My husband asked about my dreams. I told him they was nothing to worry about, and he believed me. I married a good man, see, a man what were nothing like my pa and nothing like Frank. A man whose imagination couldn't stretch further than the markers of his farmland. He were an ugly sort, some years older than me, but he were kind, and he took good care of his animals, and I knew that I'd be as happy as I could be with him.

I never saw Bonnie again, and I liked it that way. It meant that some days, when I were feeling bad, I could think that she were over there and hating her new life. Other times, I liked to think of her in a great big house with her own servants and dressed in the best gowns money could buy. Either way, I never knew the truth.

Sometimes, it's better just to dream.

EPILOGUE

Summer, 1857

I TURNED and thrust with all my strength. The metal struck against bone, a hard, cracking sound like the breaking of an eggshell. Nicholas stopped abruptly. The poker had smashed against his temple and split the skin. Blood oozed from the wound as his eyes stared vacantly at me. He dropped to his knees and fell at my feet.

After all the commotion, the sudden silence was shocking. The poker slid from my hand – for my skin had turned wet with sweat – and thudded onto the wooden floor. About me, the study was in turmoil. The chair was on its side, papers were scattered across the ground, the corner of the rug was turned over, some books had been torn off their shelves. I stood in the middle of it all, unable to move.

Barking. A door opening. Frank entered the room with Patch by his feet. The dog growled at me and jumped over Nicholas, nudging at his body.

'What have you done?' Frank prodded Nicholas with his boot. 'Jesus Christ, Bonnie. What have you done?'

Patch started barking again; the sound stabbed into my brain. 'Shut up!'

The dog barked and snarled at me. Frank crouched before the creature and held out his hand, shushed it and stroked it until it had calmed down. Then he led it out of the study and gave it a scrap of something from his pocket, and the dog ran away. Fickle.

'What happened?'

'He was going to kill me.'

'So you did it to him first? Christ!'

'What do you think I should have done?'

'Nothing. You should have just done nothing, Bonnie.' He rubbed his hand over his face. 'What should we do?'

'I'll sort it.'

'How?'

'I'll sort it, all right?' I wanted him gone. I would have said anything to make him leave so I wouldn't have to see the horror on his face whenever he looked at me. 'Please, Frank. Go back to the barn. Get your things.'

'You'll hang, Bonnie.'

'I won't.' I had promised myself I would not die for someone like Nicholas Campbell. 'Get your things and leave. I'll find you when everything is sorted.'

He fled the room. I was running over the dirt track and into Bridgefield under the light of the moon before I had even cleaned myself up.

Samuel's house was in the town on a nice street. Trees grew on the kerbsides, and the Georgian terraces had big windows and smartly painted doors. It was where the middle classes lived, and as I knocked, I had a fleeting moment of panic that a maid would answer, but then I remembered they had let their tweeny go after Samuel had been sacked.

After too many long minutes, the door creaked open. He was in his robe, and the lamp lit only half of his frowning face. When he saw me, he took my head into his hands and kissed me. I was grateful for the human contact, for his kindness. Samuel was always kind. It was that which had made me lie with him, that and greed and guilt, for I had played him like I had played everybody else when he had been the least deserving of it.

'Something awful has happened.' I sobbed against his shoulder and enjoyed the sympathy that Frank had not given me.

He dived into his house for another few moments, came out in trousers and shirtsleeves, and both of us ran to Mrs Campbell's house hand in hand.

He didn't falter when he saw the body. He took me into his arms once more and kissed my head and told me that everything would be all right.

'How? I have killed him, Samuel. The police will come for me.'

'We will tell them the truth: that you were defending yourself. Everyone knows the man is a brute.'

'They will hang me.'

'They will not. It was an accident.'

But all I could see was a set of gallows. I thought of my life in the days, the minutes, I had remaining of it.

'Samuel.' I made him look at me. I took his hand, his hand which had Nicholas's blood on it because it had been holding mine, and I placed it on my stomach. I hadn't told him. I couldn't ever find the words before, not with Frank always lingering somewhere nearby, but now I had no choice. 'I am with child.'

He stared at me, shocked, then his eyes filled with tears. He took me into his arms and kissed me, again and again, and it felt so good, and when I said I needed him, I meant it that time. I could have stayed in his embrace for years.

'Get yourself clean,' he whispered into my ear. 'Burn the dress if you must. Go to your room. When you come downstairs in the morning, raise the alarm. It will look like a robbery.'

'I don't know if I can.'

'Of course you can.' He gripped my face. We were an inch apart from each other. 'You can do it for the baby.'

I nodded. 'But you –'

'Don't worry about me. I'll sort things here. I love you, Bonnie.'

I pressed into him. All of me wanted to say it back, for wasn't he so perfect? Kind and gentle and doting – the very best of men. But my heart had never burned for him as it had burned for Frank.

'Be careful,' was all I managed to say before I prised myself away from him and walked for the door.

A noise. A grunt. I thought it had come from Samuel, but he frowned when he heard it too. Both of us turned to the body on the floor. It was no longer still. Nicholas was moving. Slowly, his hands began pushing into the floor. He was trying to get up, and he was groaning with the effort.

The dead were coming back to get me. I ran behind the desk, quaking with terror. The dead were rising …

It all happened so quickly. Samuel picked up the poker. Nicholas raised his head. For an instant, Nicholas looked at me with bloodshot eyes, and his lip curled back into a snarl, but before he could move another inch, there was that terrible sound again. Another crack, wetter this time. And then another and another. Nicholas was face down on the floor once more. His legs jerked a couple of times as Samuel smashed the poker into his skull.

'Stop!'

Samuel dropped the poker. He gasped for breath. He pushed his hair out of his face, wiped the sweat off his brow. He seemed so bewildered as he looked from Nicholas to me, so scared and childlike, that I ran to him and held him close to me.

'It will be all right,' I said, repeating his words, for I could not think of any others. 'It will be all right.' I kissed his lips and tasted Nicholas's blood. 'Stick to the plan.'

I kissed him one last time, and then I left him. I didn't know how long he stood in that study staring at the person he had just murdered; I didn't hear him leave. Upstairs in my room, I scrubbed my skin until it was speckled with bruises. I fed my gown into the fire and opened a window to air the smell. I lay on my bed and did not sleep as I thought of the body downstairs. I held on to my stomach, on to my baby.

'Everything will be all right,' I whispered to my child. I thought if I said it enough then it would come true.

I was wrong.

The baby seeped out from between my legs the night after its father swung on the end of a rope.

AFTERWORD

Thank you for taking the time to read *The Cradle Breaker.* I hope you enjoyed it, and if you would like to hear more about my work and get a **FREE** novella, *The Butcher's Wife* – which is part of the *Convenient Women* collection – then please join my mailing list by going to my website:

www.delphinewoods.com

The second novel in the *Convenient Women* collection, *The Promise Keeper,* is released September 2019.

ACKNOWLEDGMENTS

Once again, thank you, reader, for taking a chance on a new author. It means a lot!

I would also like to thank my family for being so supportive and encouraging me to follow my dreams. Thank you to my mother for always being there with constructive criticism and for being the first to read my work. Thank you to my father for all his technical support. Thank you to my fiance for believing in me completely.

Thank you to my editors at The History Quill for polishing my manuscript. To my writer friends, who share their troubles and dreams and make life as a writer less lonely - thank you! And a big thanks to the online Indie community, who share their knowledge and expertise and continue to fill our world with wonderful new books.

ABOUT THE AUTHOR

Delphine Woods graduated with a First from The Open University in 2016, where she studied for an Open Degree specialising in Creative Writing.

After a busy couple of years writing her collection of Victorian mystery-thrillers, she released her debut novella, *The Butcher's Wife,* in July 2019. *The Cradle Breaker* is the first full-length novel in the *Convenient Women* collection, and the rest of the collection will be published in the second half of 2019. These books are all set in Victorian England and have been inspired by nursery rhymes.

She lives with her fiance in Shropshire where she writes in her spare room, her dog by her feet to keep her warm. You can keep up to date with her news and get in touch with her via her newsletter and social media platforms.

For more information, visit her website:

www.delphinewoods.com

ALSO BY DELPHINE WOODS

The Butcher's Wife

A proposition of murder. A chance for freedom. But at what price?

Wolverhampton, 1862, and Nettie's husband is drunk. Again. With rent unpaid, food scarce, and money-lenders on the prowl, professional slaughterer, Russell Taylor, offers to help. But what does his devilish plan involve, and who is watching from the shadows?

As she fights for survival, Nettie must discover the real cost of life, death, truth, and lies.

The Butcher's Wife is a Victorian gothic thriller novella, part of the *Convenient Women* collection, and is available exclusively to the Delphine Woods Reader's List. It is inspired by the nursery rhyme, *Pop! Goes the Weasel,* and contains mature themes.

Available to download via my website: www.delphinewoods.com

The Promise Keeper

A game of deception. A house of secrets. A matter of life and death.

Winter 1869, and Liz Oliver must quieten her sense of unease as her brother, Tom, moves her to an isolated mansion on Devon's Jurassic coastline. There, she must live with his new, spoilt wife, Mary, and bide her time as Tom's plans begin to unfold.

But everyone is not what they appear.

As Liz and Mary struggle to hold on to their sanity, tensions build, and the past comes back to haunt them all. In this boiling pot of deceit, madness, and jealousy, who will survive?

The Promise Keeper is a stand-alone Victorian gothic mystery-thriller, the second book in the *Convenient Women* collection. This book is inspired by the nursery rhyme, *The Wise Old Owl,* and contains mature themes.

Available on Amazon from September 2019.

Printed in Great Britain
by Amazon

67097172R00135